D0051039

something to remember you by

ALSO BY GENE WILDER

What Is This Thing Called Love?
The Woman Who Wouldn't
My French Whore
Kiss Me Like A Stranger

GENE WILDER

something to remember you by

A Perilous Romance

ST. MARTIN'S PRESS ❧ NEW YORK

SOMETHING TO REMEMBER YOU BY. Copyright © 2013 by Gene Wilder. All rights reserved. Printed in the United States of America. For information, address St. Martin's Press, 175 Fifth Avenue, New York, N.Y. 10010.

www.stmartins.com

Library of Congress Cataloging-in-Publication Data

Wilder, Gene, 1935–.
  Something to Remember You By : A Perilous Romance / By Gene Wilder.—1st ed.
    p. cm.
  ISBN 978-0-312-59891-4 (hardcover)
  ISBN 978-1-250-02960-7 (e-book)
  1. World War, 1939–1945—Belgium—Fiction. 2. Soldiers—United States—Fiction. 3. Americans—Belgium—Fiction. 4. Young women—Denmark—Fiction. 5. Deception—Fiction. 6. Secrecy—Fiction. I. Title.
  PS3623.I5384S66 2013
  813'.6—dc23

2012041266

St. Martin's Press books may be purchased for educational, business, or promotional use. For information on bulk purchases, please contact Macmillan Corporate and Premium Sales Department at 1-800-221-7945 extension 5442 or write specialmarkets@macmillan.com.

First Edition: April 2013

10 9 8 7 6 5 4 3 2 1

To my friend Tom Cole,
award-winning playwright and screenwriter,
who died at seventy-five of multiple myeloma at his
home in Roxbury, Connecticut

*something to
remember you by*

ONE

Bastogne—December 25th, 1944—A white and red Christmas
At 3:00 a.m. they woke in their foxhole after the ground
shook from the explosions that had started up again. The
water in their canteens had frozen. Because of Nazi flares
the soldiers in the foxhole could see that they were surrounded by a blanket of snow. Yesterday, Cpl. Tom Cole,
their medic, poured disinfectant into the stomach wound
of Private Papales and then bandaged him, but the private was still bleeding. Their sergeant had been killed
and Privates Lancy and Eggert were bleeding from rifle
shots to their chests, their clothes wet from the snow and
their faces freezing.

At the first sign of dawn, they heard the Nazi tanks
starting to roll again.

"We'll never get out alive, will we?" Private Papales
asked softly, crying like the young boy he was. Tom Cole
held the boy's hand but didn't answer.

1

Private Steen, who had not been wounded, screamed his lungs out at the approaching tanks, as if they could hear him: "Fucking Nazis—I don't wanna die like this!"

The tanks drove back and forth over all the foxholes they could see, trying to crush the men inside, until a huge morning fog settled over the whole area. It allowed the 501st Paratroop Division to move in with their bazookas without the Nazis seeing them. When the bazookas started firing, the Nazi tanks left as fast as they could. Cheers rang out from all the scattered foxholes like a hundred-man chorus. Tom lifted himself up and thought the coast was clear enough to get his wounded men out of the stinking hole they were in. He lifted Private Papales out and laid him flat on the ground, telling him, "You're going to make it now, Timmy."

Tom went back into the foxhole and started to lift Private Lancy, who was still bleeding terribly, but a German tank suddenly came from out of nowhere and ran over Private Papales. Tom crawled up and looked at the private's crushed body and head. Tom then pushed his own head into the young boy's body and couldn't stop crying.

"Forgive me, forgive me," he whispered.

TWO

A week later, just after the overhead lights were turned off, Nurse Joy Hobbs walked down the aisle of the Brighton England Royal Army Hospital pushing a small cart as she checked on each patient and said good night to those who were still awake. When she reached Tom Cole's bed she spoke quietly.

"You look terribly sad, Tom."

"I'm all right. I'm just a little—"

"You're in pain and don't say you're not. I brought some morphine, so lie still." Joy gave Tom another injection and put the used syringe into the stainless steel tray on the cart. She looked around the room at the sleeping soldiers for a moment, and then sat down next to Tom on his bed.

"How in the world did your hip get so badly infected . . . you're a medic, aren't you?"

"One of the fellas in the foxhole was in too much pain to put his bayonet away, and I was too busy trying to stop all the bleeding around me to worry about my little scratch."

"This isn't a little scratch. And why did they make you a medic, anyway?"

"I'm a cellist, but they didn't have any room for cellists when I was drafted, and they didn't think I'd be any good in a tank or in the infantry, so they trained me to become a medic and sent me to Bastogne."

"I'm sorry. I didn't mean to offend you."

"You didn't. Have you ever been to New York, Joy?"

"I spent a glorious two weeks there, before the Nazis began bombing England. But then I wanted to go home so I worked my way as a nurse on the *Queen Elizabeth*."

"I used to live in New York before I was drafted. May I ask how old you are, Joy?"

"I'm thirty-nine, and I don't date young boys. How old are you?"

"Twenty-five," Tom said.

"Well look at that—I'm only fourteen years older than you. And when I'm sixty you'll be forty—six. Perhaps that's a little older than you thought, eh, Ducky? Tell me, do you have a girlfriend in the States?"

"Not anymore. I adored one girl and wanted to marry her, but I was very shy then, and stupid, and kept waiting to ask her to marry me until she married another guy and invited me to their wedding."

Joy leaned over and gave him a kiss on the cheek. "You'll find a girlfriend soon, of that I'm sure. Good night. Please try to sleep."

THREE

The next day, Tom received a visit from his commanding officer, Col. William Hartley.

"How's it going, son? And tell me the truth—I'm from Missouri, so don't fuck around with me."

"It's going . . . pretty rough, sir."

"Are you still in that much pain?"

"It isn't physical pain, sir. It's just that I can't get Private Papales out of my mind. He'd be alive now if I had just left him alone for five more minutes. The tanks would have been gone by then."

"Oh, you're a psychic now."

"I don't mean to whine, Colonel."

"Then don't whine. You're putting all your eggs in the wrong basket, son. If you hadn't tried to get those boys out of that foxhole they would have bled to death, and you would have been a pretty rotten medic. Yes?"

"I know, sir."

"No, you don't know. Grow up! You don't seem to

know the difference between a hero and a jerk. Listen to me: I'm giving you a one-week convalescent leave beginning next week, but I want to put you to work right after that. You're smart, and I like smart soldiers. And you're damn brave, so I'm promoting you to lieutenant junior grade. I was thinking about the Intelligence Service for you, but tell me if you think there's something you'd be better at. Clear?"

FOUR

On the morning of January 14th, Joy said, "Excuse me, Lieutenant, sir, but you just received your new army uniform this morning, with a beautiful Eisenhower jacket."

"How could they know my exact size?"

"Because I told them. And here's a letter to you from the Home Office. I wonder if they're going to make you a colonel this time."

Tom opened the letter and read it out loud:

LT. THOMAS COLE
ROYAL ARMY HOSPITAL
BRIGHTON ENGLAND

Dear Lieutenant Cole,
You have been granted a one-week convalescent leave—
January 15th until January 21st—but please report to
Colonel Hartley at 1300 hours on the afternoon of
January 18th for a brief visit. The address is 1408

Whitehall, London. There are a series of tunnels, sir. His
office just says COL. H *on the door.*

Best wishes,
Sgt. John Morris
Asst. to Col. William Hartley

"Well, aren't you the cat's meow?" Joy said. "Your commanding officer certainly sounds like a good man. You want to hear my advice?"

"Of course."

"Leave your brain alone for a while, Tom. Go to London and see some shows. Some of them will make you laugh, which is what you need right now."

"They're putting on plays even with the bombing?"

"Absolutely. If the bombing gets bad the people in the audience can rush down to the Tube if they want, but the actors still continue on with the play, regardless."

"I wonder what the people in New York would do if the bombing ever happened to them?"

"They'd run down to the subway station, Ducky."

AFTER LUNCH, Joy handed Tom a list of plays to choose from. She underlined *Strike It Again*, with Norman Wisdom. "Mandy Adams is my cousin and she has a house on Lower Sloane Street and she's got a nice room for you, free of charge if you want it."

"Why free of charge?"

"Because she's my cousin."

"And you told her what a charmer I am."

"Something like that. But she's married, so be careful."

"Where do I go and how do I get there?"

"Here's her address and phone number. Take the Express train to London Victoria station, which is just one hour flat, and then a cab. Mandy's expecting you tomorrow morning between ten and eleven. And after you and Mandy say hello and have a nice hot cup of tea with a scone she'll have made, take a cab to the Prince of Wales Theatre to see Norman Wisdom. The Shepherdess Café is right around the corner if you want to eat something after the show. Matinee is at two-thirty, and I'm sure it'll be crowded, so get there early."

"How early do I have to be at the theater to buy a ticket?"

"It's already reserved for you, Lieutenant Thomas Cole."

"Thanks, Mom."

FIVE

Tom put his duffel bag into the small, but very pleasant, room that Mandy showed him. She was warm and friendly, just like Joy, and after they had their tea and scone together Tom washed up, combed his hair, and got into the waiting taxi that Mandy had called. He waved a thank-you kiss to her as the taxi drove off.

When he arrived at Coventry Street the cabbie stuck his arm out and pointed: "Right there, sir." Tom paid him and walked quickly to the box office of the Prince of Wales Theatre. As he started to take out his wallet the attendant said, "It's on us today, Lieutenant. God bless ya," and handed Tom his ticket.

What in the world did Joy tell that man, Tom wondered.

Strike It Again was a wonderful show, and he loved watching Norman Wisdom sing and dance, but Tom couldn't bring himself to laugh. He kept picturing his life in the foxhole only a few months ago, helping men who were bleeding to death and seeing that tank crush Private Papales's guts out, and here he was watching an entertainer make people all around him laugh their guts out.

SIX

When the show was over, Tom walked around the corner to 33 Coventry Street and through a door with long, overlapping curtains, which were used to keep any light from getting out. All the windows inside the Shepherdess Café were covered with pretty curtains that hid the thick black curtains behind them, almost exactly the way he saw them in Brighton Hospital every evening, to keep Nazi bombers from seeing the lights.

Now that Tom was inside he thought that the Shepherdess Café was charming. It was lit only with candles and a pianist was playing popular wartime songs, mostly ones that Vera Lynn made popular. On one of the walls there was a reproduction of a well-known portrait of King George VI in his dress uniform. Everyone was dressed warmly. Most of the women were wearing cardigans and shawls, and all of the men wore neckties and sweaters under their jackets. This was January, after all.

A few yards in front of Tom there was a young woman

sitting alone at a very small table. The café was so packed that, despite how hungry he was and how wonderful the smells emanating through the room were, Tom turned and started walking toward the entrance to get away from the crowd. Suddenly, from out of nowhere, a short, middle-aged man, wearing black trousers, a white shirt, and a cloth apron, started pulling Tom toward the small table with the young woman, who was still alone.

With a strong cockney accent, the waiter said loudly, "Please, sir, this way if you don't mind, sir, and I have a nice seat for you right here at this lovely little table with this lovely young woman and I'll be back quick as a wink," he said in one long breath as he handed Tom a huge menu and almost tripped over his own feet as he hurried away.

"Oh, waiter," the young woman called out, but he was already halfway across the room by the time she said it.

Seeing her up close, Tom was taken with how lovely she was. Hers was a simple loveliness. She had the fresh skin and raspberry cheeks of a child and beautiful long auburn hair with a pink bow in it.

"I'm sorry for intruding," Tom said. "But would you mind very much if I share this tiny table with you? It's actually an order from your waiter, and since I'm a soldier I have to obey orders," Tom said, hoping that he wasn't coming on too strongly.

"Of course, please do. I was only trying to tell the waiter what I wanted to eat," she said with a little laugh, and with an accent that Tom couldn't determine. "I can't see for sure in this light, but are you a captain?"

"Thank you for the promotion, but I'm just a lieutenant. My name is Tom Cole, and I'm making a guess that you're Swedish?"

"Very close. I'm Danish. My name is Anna Rosenkilde."

"And do you prefer if I call you Miss or Mrs. Rosenkilde?"

A smile played upon her lips as if she were quite used to young soldiers coming on to her. "Since you're American I'm sure you would prefer to just call me Anna . . . is that right?"

"Well . . . yes, I guess I would. Have you studied this gigantic menu, Anna?"

"I have."

"And do you know what you want?"

"I do."

"I'm not very familiar with London restaurants," Tom said, "so please tell me what you're going to have and then I can just say, 'The same for me, please.'"

"Certainly. I am going to have sautéed octopus with some raw tuna to begin," Anna said.

"Well, maybe I *should* take a peek at the menu," Tom said.

Anna began giggling. "I'm sorry, Lieutenant. That was a joke. We Danish are jokers, you know. Now I tell you the truth; I'm having Dover sole with roasted potatoes . . . if our waiter should come back."

"I suppose I can either laugh or cry, falling for that one," Tom said.

"I don't like crying, Lieutenant, so if I have a choice, would you please laugh?"

Tom tried his hardest to laugh, but it wouldn't come out. He kept making the strangest sounds, which made Anna laugh out loud. The crowd sitting nearby turned to look at Tom and started giggling themselves, which made Anna laugh louder. Pretty soon the whole café started laughing. Tom looked at the crowd laughing at him and suddenly burst out laughing so hard that tears began to pour out of his eyes.

"Thank you, Anna," Tom said as he wiped his eyes. "I haven't laughed in a long time."

"It's good to laugh. Good for your liver, good for your heart. So now, Lieutenant—what shall we do about our waiter? Should we just not wait any longer?"

"No, ma'am, we're both starving," Tom said as he got up and walked through the crowd and straight into the open kitchen where he saw at least eight or nine people cooking food while others were washing or drying dishes.

Tom shouted so loud that the pianist stopped playing and the whole café could hear him: "My name is Lieutenant Thomas Cole and I've just come back from Bastogne, Belgium, where I was fighting the Nazis with my English friends. My lovely date and I are starving, so please, could we have two orders of Dover sole with roasted potatoes and a little white wine?"

Silence for a moment, and then one of the kitchen staff started singing, "For He's a Jolly Good Fellow." Then the rest of the staff joined in. By the second round, everyone in the café joined in as they applauded Tom.

Tom became so embarrassed that he lowered his head as he walked back to Anna, shaking hands with most of the men in the crowd who wished him, "God bless you, son," and getting hugs from several of the women. When he finally arrived at Anna's table he said, "I don't know what got into me."

Anna got up and gave him a hug. "You are also *my* hero, Tom," she said, calling him "Tom" for the first time, and giving him a kiss on the cheek.

"Oh, my, thank you," Tom said. "Was that just because I made a fool of myself hollering my lungs out, or was the little kiss because I called you my lovely date?"

"No, you silly, it was for getting us our dinner," Anna said, giggling at her joke.

SEVEN

After they had finished eating and were sipping the last of their bottle of wine, Anna said, "What did you do before the war, Tom?"

"I lived in New York and I played the cello fairly well, but I decided that I wanted to become a conductor—not a train conductor, Anna—"

Anna burst out laughing.

"A musical conductor. So I moved to Los Angeles, California, in 1941, and I studied at UCLA with Arnold Schoenberg."

"Oh, how wonderful," Anna said.

"Yes, but then I was drafted and they made me a medic. And now—may I please ask you one very simple question?"

"Of course," she said.

"When did you come to London and how did you get here and do you have a job here and where do you live?"

"You are a funny man. All right, I tell you a little bit. First of all, I'm Jewish."

"So am I," Tom said.

"Well, in 1943 Hitler ordered all Danish Jews to be arrested and deported to a concentration camp. He did the same thing the year before in Norway, sending Jews to Auschwitz, but it was different with us. The Germans were supposed to take us by surprise during Rosh Hashanah, but when we arrived for services the rabbi told us not to go home that night. Some of us hid in the morgues in the hospital, some waited in the woods. About eighty Jews were caught hiding in the loft of a church and were betrayed by a young Danish girl who was in love with a German soldier. But the Danish Resistance and ordinary citizens started evacuating almost eight thousand of us to Sweden in fishing boats. When the Nazis suspected how we were leaving they began using police dogs to inspect the boats before they left, but our scientists developed a powder of rabbits' blood and cocaine. They put it on handkerchiefs and gave them to the captains of the boats. The dogs were attracted to the rabbits' blood but the cocaine ruined their sense of smell, so they couldn't find us hiding in the boats."

"That was brilliant."

"And when we made it to Sweden, the RAF flew those of us who wanted to go to the UK to fight against the Germans. We flew to Scotland. I took a train to London, got a job with the Women's Auxiliary Air Force of the RAF, and now I wear a pretty blue uniform when I'm on duty."

"I admire you."

"And I admire you, Lieutenant Tom, for what you must have been through."

"The only thing you left out is where you live."

"I live on the third floor of a house on Bywater Street in Chelsea. It's a quiet cul-de-sac just off King's Road. My landlady is wonderful and the rent is so little. Her husband died during the Blitz and if I'm home when the bombing starts Bertie always holds my hand when she sees that I'm scared."

"Anna, I'm on a week's convalescent leave right now and then they're going to put me to work again. I'm not sure where, so, may I come visit you while I'm still in London? I mean, visit you where you work or we could go to a movie? I'd be very lonely if I couldn't see you again."

"I'd be happy to see you again, but I think it would be better if we met here in the café. Seven o'clock tomorrow evening? That's when I get off work—if that's all right with you?"

"Sure, but how do I call you, just in case?"

"No, don't call me 'Just in Case,' call me 'Anna,'" she said, unable to stifle a giggle.

EIGHT

The next evening Tom walked into the Shepherdess Café at a quarter to seven. Since he had become somewhat of a celebrity the night before, their Cockney waiter, who was a foot shorter than Tom, greeted him with a warm hug. "I was hopin' ta see you again, Guv, and here you are. Isn't life funny? Is the young lady joining us?"

"Yes, she's going to join us at seven."

"Brilliant," the waiter said. "I got a lovely little table for you right here." When Tom sat down, the pianist began playing, "I'll See You Again" and nodded to him. Tom nodded back.

"Sorry we haven't got the Sancerre anymore, Guv, but I got a lovely bottle of this Moroccan white that I'm told is just like the Sancerre. I'll keep it in the ice bucket right here beside you so's you and the lady can have it whenever you're ready," and off he went.

It wasn't as crowded this night as it was the night before, but people were still coming in. Anna didn't arrive at 7, or 7:15, but at 7:25 she rushed in, out of breath, but smiling.

"Sorry, Tom, they gave me a little extra work and then it was so so cold and dark outside. I hope you weren't worried about my not coming?"

"No, I was just anxious to see you again." As he helped Anna into her chair he said, "Our favorite waiter brought us a bottle of Moroccan white wine. He hears that it's just as good as the Sancerre. Are you ready to try it?"

"Oh, yes. Please."

Tom took the bottle out of the ice bucket and poured both of them half a glass. As they clicked Tom said, "Cheers," and Anna said, "Skal."

After a swallow Anna asked, "What do you think?"

"Well, I wouldn't say it's as good as Sancerre, but it's not bad, considering that we're in the middle of a war. What did you do at work today?"

"I shot radio beams into the air."

"Radio beams?"

"Yes. And then I watch to see if they hit any airplanes. If they didn't, I keep watching. But if I see a blip on my radar, then I wait for a signal that it's one of our planes."

"And if it isn't?"

"Then I tell my boss and up go the RAF. What did you do today?"

"Oh, what I did was much more complicated than that. I went to the Tate Museum and the British Museum and the National Gallery and had a cucumber sandwich and a cup of tea and then went to St. Paul's Cathedral and the Royal Academy of Music, and then I went to a foot doctor."

"You silly, you make more jokes than I do. I think you must have Danish blood in you."

"Probably from all the Danish pastry I've eaten."

"Do you really like Danish pastry, Tom?"

"Very much, especially if it's from New York."

"Now you're just playing games with me. What do you want for dinner?" Anna asked with a big smile.

"Just to be with you and to eat a nice big steak, if they have it."

"You feel better tonight, don't you?"

"Yes I do. And here comes our waiter!"

"Good evenin' to ya, m'lady. Nice to see ya both again. Now then, what're we havin' for dinner tonight and how was the Moroccan white wine?"

"May I ask what your name is?" Tom asked.

"Alfred, sir. Alfred Hollingberry. But you can just call me Alfred if ya don't mind, Guv, 'cause you'll forget Hollingberry in an hour."

"Well, the wine was good, Alfred. Thank you very much. As for our dinner . . . what do you feel like, Anna?"

"Right now I feel like someone's warm hand," she said, "and then I think I'll just have some grilled salmon, if you have it?"

22

"I do, ma'am. Lovely! And, sir?"

"I would really like a steak if you have it," Tom said.

"You could have a wonderful *Vienna* steak, Guv, and it comes with roast potatoes, and you can have a very good bottle of Moroccan merlot with it. How's that sound?"

"What in the world is a Vienna steak?"

"Well to tell ya the truth, Guv, it's really just ground meat, like your American hamburger, but it's mixed with pieces of bread and some wonderful spices and they cook it just right. If you want a *real* steak I'm afraid that's almost impossible, except maybe in one of those hoity-toity posh restaurants."

"Don't worry, Alfred, I'll be very happy with—" but before Tom could finish his sentence the air raid siren rang loudly, modulating back and forth from a high pitch to a low one.

"Steady as she goes, folks!" Alfred shouted. "You can go right 'round the corner to the Tube," he said as he ran off to help his customers.

The crowd around Tom and Anna may have been nervous, but most of them stayed in their seats. A few got up and headed quickly for the Piccadilly Tube station.

"Are you all right, Anna?"

"Thank you, yes. I should be used to it by now. It's just knowing that the bombs are coming."

"Do you want me to take you to the Piccadilly station?"

23

"I'd rather stay here with you, if that's all right. It gets so crowded down there, and the smell isn't very pleasant. Many of the people sleep there all night. Cots are provided for them. Tell me . . . tell me who your favorite composers are."

"Rachmaninov, Chopin, Schubert, and probably—"

The first bomb exploded about half a mile away. There was silence for a few seconds and then a mighty explosion was heard from a bomb that landed much closer. Tom saw Anna's eyes tighten and reached for her hand. She looked up and gave him a smile. "Thank you, Bertie," she said simply.

"You're welcome. I wanted to hold your hand anyway."

"It's funny," Anna said. "I'm actually very brave. I'm not afraid of very many things, not even when the Nazis were searching for us, but I'm just not used to bombs. When I hear that horrible sound I suddenly feel that my life and everything I love is going to end."

"How many of your radio beams hit some planes today?"

"I . . . I don't know, I think . . . I was . . . Tom, would you like Bertie's address and telephone number? I mean, just in case you can't find me?"

"Absolutely. Do you have a pen?"

"Yes, but no paper," Anna said, handing him her pen.

"This tablecloth is just plain brown paper," Tom said as he tore off a small piece. "Okay, I'm ready!"

"Eighty-four Bywater Street. The phone number is Flaxen 399, but you just have to dial FLA and then the number. Bertie's name is Cresswell . . . oh, but she's gone to visit her sister for the weekend."

"Never mind," Tom said as he put the piece of paper into his jacket pocket. "There, now I'll never lose you."

A flurry of bombs landed nearby. Anna squeezed Tom's hand but kept looking at him, trying to smile.

FORTY-FIVE MINUTES later the "all clear" sounded. Anna and Tom were still holding hands when Alfred came bouncing up to them with the bottle of Moroccan merlot he promised. "Here ya are, Guv. Not too late, I hope. The salmon and the Vienna steak will be along in a jiff."

AFTER THEIR dinner Anna stood up slowly. Tom got up and stood next to her. "I'd better go home now, Tom. Thank you so much for holding my hand when I was frightened," Anna said and gave him a quick kiss. He looked into her eyes for several seconds, then held her face gently in his hands and gave her a long kiss. Anna broke into a huge smile. "Oh, goodness," she said. "I'm so glad you did that."

"Anna, I'm not going to let you go home alone when it's so dark outside, and cabs will be scarce. I'm at Lower Sloane Street, almost around the corner from you, so I'll walk you home."

"Thank you," she said, obviously relieved.

When Tom took out his wallet Anna said, "No, we have to go Dutch."

"You're not Dutch, you're Danish, so don't talk silly." Anna beamed.

Tom paid the bill, and they both said good night to Alfred, who said, "See ya soon and thanks for the lovely tip."

"See you soon," they both answered as they walked out of the café holding hands.

NINE

It wasn't as cold outside as they thought it would be, it was almost balmy compared to the last few days. The streetlamps wouldn't be turned on till dawn, but the curbs were painted white since so many people had injured themselves falling off of them. All the cars had their headlights masked with only a slit of light allowed. Tom held Anna's hand as they walked slowly and talked about Copenhagen and New York and Danish pastry and music.

"I play the violin," Anna said, "but I get so confused when I try to play Schoenberg. I just don't understand him."

"Well, I spent six months studying with him in Los Angeles until I was drafted, but his twelve-tone technique and atonal compositions made me dizzy, if that's any comfort to you. I knew he was a genius, but at the same time I longed for Rachmaninov and Chopin and the major-minor scale system. I suppose it's like painting . . . What's beautiful?"

"I was the same as you," Anna said. "Some pieces are so beautiful that they make me cry, and others . . . well, they give me a headache, so I don't play them anymore."

Tom didn't speak for what seemed like a long minute, then he said: "Anna . . . I was very brave when I was surrounded by the Nazis in Bastogne, but to tell you the truth, I'm actually quite shy, at least with women—except when I saw you for the first time at that little table in the café, with that pretty pink bow in your hair. May I ask you something personal?"

"Yes, I think so," she said.

"Have you ever really loved anyone?"

"Do you mean, have I ever been in love?"

"Yes."

"Well, I thought I was once, about three years ago. I was only twenty years old, and I was very immature, about physical love at least. I don't know what I expected him to do, or me to do, and I realized pretty soon that it wasn't love at all that I felt. I mean not being in love. Did you have many girlfriends, Tom . . . and have you ever been in love?"

"I had one girlfriend who I thought I loved and I really wanted to marry her. But I waited so long before I had the courage to propose to her that she married someone else. After awhile I realized how lucky I was, because she didn't care for music or theater or ballet or opera, or making love . . . so we had nowhere to go but down. I'm a grateful twenty-five year old now." Tom stopped when he saw Bywater Street.

" Oh, no! Here's your street already. Now I don't know what to say, because . . . I don't want to leave you," Tom said as he searched Anna's blue-green eyes.

Anna put her arms around him and hugged him. "But you've already said it, don't you know that? Come with me. No one's home and I have a lovely room with a nice shower."

ANNA HELD Tom's hand and led him to the third floor and opened the door. It was a quietly beautiful room with heavy rose-colored curtains and a blue bedspread. The window didn't have a blackout shade but with the curtains covering it no light sneaked out from the only light in the room, which was from a little lamp next to Anna's bed.

"Please make yourself comfortable. I'm just going to go into the bathroom to wash up a bit and then put in my little cup. I'll be out in a few minutes. Don't go away," she said with a smile.

Tom saw a small bookcase on one of the walls. Most of

the books were in Danish, but quite a few were in English and French. He took a glance at the French and English titles as he took off his jacket and shirt.

Candide—Voltaire
   subtitled: "A classic case of optimism in the face of all
      odds" *In English.*
The Count of Monte Cristo—Alexandre Dumas. *In English.*
Uncle Tom's Cabin—Harriet Beecher Stowe. *In English.*
Tom Sawyer—Mark Twain. *In English.*

Anna's closet was partially open and the scent that came from it was wonderful. Anna stepped out of the bathroom wearing a pretty lavender robe.

"Your turn, dear," she said. "I'll get us each a small glass of Lillet. Do you like Lillet?"

"If you like it, I'm sure I will. I'll be right back.

After Tom washed up, he came out wearing his underwear, shoes, and socks, and carrying a bath towel. Anna was lying in bed under the covers. Tom sat down on the bed beside her and took off his shoes and socks. "Are you ready for me to come into bed with you?"

"I am very ready," she said. Tom took off his underwear and slipped into bed beside her.

"Take a sip of Lillet with me," she said as she handed Tom his glass.

"Skal," she said.

"Cheers," he said as they clicked glasses and tasted their drink.

"I like it," Tom said and then kissed her.

"I hope you will like me, too," Anna said.

Tom put his glass down and put his arm under Anna's head, then placed his naked body against hers.

"Could we stay like this for a little while?" Anna said. "It's so comforting."

"Of course we can," Tom said as he touched Anna's remarkably smooth face and kissed her lips in a way that did not necessarily ask her to become aroused. But when she squeezed him closer he caressed her breasts, kissing each one as if he were still kissing her lips. When Anna pulled him closer with a deep sigh he ran his hand slowly over her belly and along her thigh. They held each other side by side for several minutes until Anna said, "Oh, please, would you come inside me now?" When he did, her face became filled with tears and they both reached bliss. They held each other side by side for three or four minutes, then rolled over onto their backs and talked for almost half an hour, sipping their Lillet and making each other laugh.

"I'd better leave now," Tom said. "You have to work tomorrow."

Tom got dressed. Anna put on her robe and walked him downstairs. He kissed her again and then felt her tears falling onto his nose. "Anna, why are you still crying?"

"Because I don't know when I'll see you again," she answered.

"But we'll see each other tomorrow night, won't we?"

"Of course, dear. Seven o'clock," she said wiping her tears.

They kissed each other again and then Tom left.

TEN

The guard who checked Tom's I.D. at the entrance said, "The walkway is over a mile long, sir, and it's all underground, so please look carefully at the names on the doors so you don't get lost."

Tom walked slowly along the walkway until he saw Col. H on one of the doors. He walked into a room filled with officers sitting at a long table with maps on it. A major, who was doing the talking, looked up when he saw Tom and said, "What're you looking for, Lieutenant?"

"I'm looking for Colonel Hartley, sir."

"Just knock on that door to your left," the major said and then turned back to the other officers. Tom walked to the door and knocked. He heard someone inside say, "Come in!"

A sergeant was sitting behind a small desk, typing. When he looked up he asked, "Are you Lieutenant Cole, sir?"

"Yes, I'm a little early."

"Quite all right, sir. I'm Sergeant Morris," he said as he stood up quickly. "I'm the one who wrote that letter to you from Colonel Hartley. I'll tell the colonel that you're here."

A second later Tom heard, "Bring him in!" and Tom was ushered into the colonel's office. Colonel Hartley was standing. Tom saluted quickly, but the colonel said, "You don't have to do that in here, Cole." He gave Tom a warm handshake. "I'm glad to see you, son."

"Thank you, sir."

"Let's sit over here on these comfy chairs." As Tom walked toward the chairs he saw photos, which he guessed were the colonel's wife and children on the colonel's desk. There were no windows, of course, since the office was underground.

"Would you like a nice hot cup of tea, as the English say every day of their lives?"

"Thank you, sir, no. I just had lunch." After they both sat down, Colonel Hartley looked at Tom's eyes for the longest time, as if he were deciding how to say something.

"You're Jewish," he finally said.

"Are you asking me, sir, or . . ."

"No, I'm telling you. I know quite a bit about you, Cole. You also speak fluent German, don't you?"

"Yes, sir. My father was from Austria and he was Jewish, but he left when Hitler blamed the Jews for Germany losing the First World War. I think he knew what was coming. He went to Chicago to study medicine, met my mother, who was French and studying music, and then they had me."

"I would like to have known your father. I didn't know very much about your mother, but she must have been a great inspiration for you to become a cellist."

"She was, sir."

"Tell me something, Cole . . . have you ever heard of a German named Heinrich Müller?"

". . . I don't think so."

"He's a policeman. A brilliant policeman, actually. He became the head of the State Police in Nazi Germany, then became the head of the Gestapo and signed orders requiring the immediate delivery to Auschwitz of forty-five thousand Jews for extermination. He was Adolf Eichmann's immediate superior. Are you sure you wouldn't like a cup of tea?"

The two men stared at each other. Tom looked slightly pale.

"Yes, I would like a cup of tea, sir."

Colonel Hartley got up and used his intercom. "Two cups of tea please, Morris." He stayed standing while he talked. "Have you given any thought to my suggestion that you work in Intelligence?"

"I have, sir, to the extent that I know what it is. I mean, I'm just a soldier—you can order me to do anything you want—but what does the Intelligence Service mean, apart from my having to be fairly intelligent?"

"Well, for instance, you might have to interrogate captured enemies. Of course you'd have to speak the language perfectly. In your case, if they were German that wouldn't be a problem. Do you speak French, Tom?"

"I speak it very well, sir. My mother didn't want her language to be pushed out of the way by my father."

"Good for her. You'd also have to convert English into Morse code and Morse code into English, and you'd have to know how to deceive an enemy, and you'd have to be able to perform under physical and mental pressures. But eventually . . . you'd be judged by your ability to make decisions on your own."

There was a quiet knock on the door and Sergeant Morris walked in with the tea. He placed the tray on the small table in front of Colonel Hartley and left quickly.

"Please help yourself, Cole. The little cookies are very good. They call them 'biscuits' here." While they were both sipping their tea Colonel Hartley said, "By the way, Heinrich Müller is now a lieutenant general. Do you know how to say that in German?"

"He's a *Gruppenführer.*"

"Thanks. I get mixed up trying to pronounce some of those goddamn names. Well, this swine is a workaholic. Never takes a holiday. He was the chief architect of the plan to exterminate all Jews in Europe."

"Colonel, are you going to ask me to find Müller and shoot him?"

"No, not at all," the colonel said. "I just thought you might want to seek revenge the way I do. By the way, have you ever jumped out of an airplane?"

"Not without a parachute."

The colonel smiled. "Good for you. I deserved that. Of course, there'd be a dozen tests you'd have to go through, which I'm sure you'd pass easily enough, but there's no point in my ordering you to go into Intelligence if you don't want to."

"You already knew I would or you wouldn't have asked me, sir."

Colonel Hartley nodded a slow "yes."

"By the way, if you don't mind my asking, do you have a sweetheart here in London?"

"Yes, sir. I care for her very much. She's a lovely woman—Danish, and also Jewish. She escaped Denmark in a fishing boat that took her to Sweden. Now, she works right here, in one of those tunnels where they shoot radio waves into the sky to locate German planes."

"The Radar tunnel is three doors down from here, on the right-hand side. You'd better get going, Cole."

"Thank you, sir."

TOM HURRIED down the thin walkway until he saw the door with RADAR printed on it. When he entered the

room he saw a middle-aged lady in a blue WAAF uniform signing a stack of papers. She looked up when Tom
walked toward her.

"Yes, Lieutenant, can I help you?" the lady asked.

"Yes, I'm looking for a young lady named Anna Rosenkilde. She works here with you."

"I'm terribly sorry, Lieutenant, we have no one here by
that name."

"Well . . . I mean, isn't this where you send radio waves
into the sky?" Tom said with a little laugh.

"My name is Sally Bedloe. I've worked here for eight
years and I assure you that we have no one with that
name. I think you must have heard some of our younger
girls talking at lunchtime. Yes, we send radio waves into
the sky, but I'm not allowed to talk about it. Did your
young lady friend say that she worked in Radar?"

"Well . . . she didn't mention the word 'Radar.'"

"Did she mention my name, Sally Bedloe?"

"No, she never mentioned any name, but I think you
must have seen her at some time. She's twenty-three years
old, she's Danish and has a slight accent. She's a WAAF
in the RAF and wears a blue uniform just like yours. You
must have seen her."

A pilot, who had been on the phone when Tom came
in, walked over after he hung up and stood next to Sally
Bedloe. "The woman you've mentioned doesn't work

here. We're quite busy right now. You'd best try some other tunnel, Lieutenant."

Tom saw that the pilot was a captain. "Sorry, sir," he said, and walked out. He hurried back to Colonel Hartley's office.

After he told Sergeant Morris the circumstances, the sergeant said, "Wait outside, sir. I'll come and get you when the colonel is free."

Tom sat in the room with all the maps and officers. After half an hour, Colonel Hartley popped his head out of his office. "That lady is Sally Bedloe and she's a crackerjack. Knows her stuff. I'm in the middle of a pile of things right now, so if you don't hear from me in an hour, go home, and call Sergeant Morris tomorrow."

The colonel went back into his office. Tom waited for an hour and then went to the Shepherdess.

ELEVEN

Tom waited in the café for almost an hour. As soon as Alfred came by to top up his glass of wine, Tom said, "I'm getting a little worried, Alfred. She told me seven and it's almost eight o'clock. Is there a phone I can use?"

"Yes, Guv, in the manager's office, right over there on your left. It's not locked."

"I won't be long, but if my lady friend should walk in, please don't let her leave. Just bring her to me."

"You bet, Guv."

When Tom got inside the office he took out the piece of brown paper in his wallet that had Mrs. Bertie Cresswell's telephone number and address on it. He dialed.

"Hello, Mrs. Cresswell, this is Lieutenant Tom Cole. I'm calling because I was supposed to meet Anna here tonight, at the café we've been going to, and I've been waiting here for almost an hour, and . . . Anna! Anna Rosenkilde! . . . What do you mean you never heard of her?

You must have heard of her, she lives in your house . . . Hello . . . Hello, Mrs. Cresswell, can you hear me?"

TOM TOOK a cab to Mandy Adams's house. Just as he arrived, the air raid siren sounded. Mandy pulled him into the living room and pulled down the rest of the curtains over the windows. "Now then, Romeo, how romantic to be wooing and cooing a young woman just before the bombs arrive? Where is your lovely? At home, I hope."

"You're just like your cousin, did you know that, Mandy?"

"I've heard it before. Are you complaining?"

"Not at all," Tom said. "But my 'lovely,' as you call her, never showed up at the café. And the lady where she works said she never heard of her. When I called the house where Anna lives, the sweet lady who owns the house said she also never heard of her."

TWELVE

The next morning Tom stood nervously in front of Colonel Hartley.

"Tell me what's the matter."

"I think I'm going slightly crazy, sir, and I don't know what to do. I met Anna in a café in London and I liked her right away. She made me laugh and I made her laugh and after a while I fell in love with her, but she lied to me about her work and shooting rays up to the sky. Sally Bedloe said she never saw or heard of Anna Rosenkilde. Anna and I were supposed to meet last night at the Shepherdess Café and suddenly she disappears, without saying a word to me. I was afraid she might have gotten hurt in an air raid, so I called Anna's landlady, who Anna loved and said she lived with, and the landlady said that she never heard of her. I'm not even sure who Anna is anymore or who she's really working for."

"Why don't you sit down, Tom?"

"I'd rather stand, if you don't mind, Colonel."

"I do mind, Lieutenant Cole. Sit down."

Tom sat in one of the chairs next to the colonel's desk. Colonel Hartley stood in front of him and said, "Have you ever heard of the SOE?"

"No, sir."

"It means Special Operations Executive . . . also known as Churchill's Secret Army. Its mission is to help facilitate sabotage behind enemy lines, and you need good agents to do that."

"Are you telling me that Anna Rosenkilde is one of your agents?"

"I'm not talking about Anna Rosenkilde. I'd be breaking rules if I did. I'm just saying that the primary quality required of an agent is a deep knowledge of the country he or she is supposed to operate in, especially their language, which is essential if this person is supposed to pass as a native of that country. I don't know if or where your friend is right now, and I'm terribly busy with so many other things, but if you were working in the Intelligence Service you might know more about these things than I do. Would you like a nice hot cup of tea, Lieutenant?"

"I certainly would, sir."

THIRTEEN

On his first day of Intelligence training Tom was taken to Ringway Airfield, near Manchester, where he had to parachute from a plane at an altitude of five hundred feet. It was a refresher course for Tom, since he had gone through this before in the States, training as a medic. Before lunch he had to jump again, this time from four hundred feet. That evening, when it was dark, he had to jump at three hundred feet, which would be the height and time of day most likely to occur if he were in action.

At the end of that day Tom walked casually up to his SOE boss, Capt. David Pryce. Hoping to catch him off guard he said, "Oh, I almost forgot, sir—how is my friend, Anna Rosenkilde, doing?"

"Is she Jewish?" Captain Pryce asked.

"Yes, sir, but why would you ask a question like that?"

"We would never send a Jewish man or woman back to Denmark. They tried to kill almost all the Jews in Denmark—didn't you know that?"

"I knew it very well, sir. She told me."

"I see. Well the only Danish woman we have working with us is Helena Simonsen, and she's not Jewish."

"Can you tell me what she looks like?"

"I cannot."

"I see. Thank you, sir."

AFTER HE was flown back to London Tom decided to visit Bertie Cresswell that night instead of trying to call her on the phone again. When he rang the doorbell a very pleasant-looking lady, somewhere in her fifties, opened the door.

"Mrs. Cresswell?"

"Yes."

"Please listen to me for just one minute. I was in your home a few days ago, with Anna Rosenkilde. I didn't see you because she told me you were visiting your sister over the weekend. Anna told me how wonderful you are and how you used to hold her hand when the bombs were falling. Mrs. Cresswell, I'm terribly fond of Anna, and I think she's very fond of me. I found out that she might actually be back in Denmark right now."

Mrs. Cresswell stared at Tom, but didn't try to interrupt.

"Bertie—if I may call you that—does the name 'Simonsen' mean anything to you? Helena Simonsen?"

"That was the name of her French teacher's sister," Bertie said.

"French teacher?"

"Yes, they were very close, but Anna told me she was afraid to even say good-bye to her when she left."

"Why?"

"Miss Simonsen wasn't Jewish. Anna said she couldn't take a chance of anyone hearing about the Jews escaping. I'm sorry what I did to you on the telephone, Mr.—"

"Tom Cole. Lieutenant Tom Cole."

"Anna told me many times that if she should ever disappear for a while, to not tell anyone where she is or who she is. No one. I'm sorry, Lieutenant."

"You did the right thing. And please just call me Tom."

"Thank you."

"Are you all right, Bertie? Do you need anything?"

"I'm fine. Please take care of yourself, Tom."

FOURTEEN

The next day, on eighteen acres of an old English Manor house, Tom's training focused on how to deal with armed SS troops and military patrols. He also learned how to use a handheld walkie-talkie using very high radio frequencies, which enabled him to transmit intelligence to planes flying above him without detection by German shortwave radio operators. On the lunch break Tom went up to Captain Pryce and asked, "Sir, can you at least tell me if Miss Simonsen is all right?"

"I'm not allowed to talk about any of our agents, Lieutenant Cole."

Tom walked away, mumbling, "Secrets and more goddamn secrets."

After lunch, it was so cold inside and outside that Captain Pryce held a meeting with Tom and the other newcomers to SOE in the library of the manor house where a warm fireplace was waiting for them. At four o'clock that afternoon Captain Pryce said: "Why don't we take a break, so you gentlemen can have your foursies."

Tom looked puzzled, wondering if "foursies" wasn't the British way of saying, "You can take a pee break now." Alex, the English lieutenant sitting next to him, saw Tom's puzzled look and said, "Elevensies and foursies just means it's teatime, old bean. You can also smoke if you want."

Tom whispered, "Thanks," and then stood up with the other men who headed for the tea-and-coffee trolley that had been wheeled into the library.

FIFTEEN

At 7:45 p.m. "Helena Simonsen" parachuted three hundred feet into the darkness and landed on the Amager Beach Park, near Copenhagen's city center. After burying her parachute, she took out her new passport and Danish government I.D. from her backpack and put them into her warm jacket pocket. She wanted to have them ready for the men of the Danish Resistance who were going to meet her: she knew she would have to show proof that she was the agent they were expecting. It was a freezing cold night. While she waited, she could see, far off in the distance, the tiny lights on the coast of Sweden.

After seven or eight minutes she saw a flashlight coming toward her. When three men arrived, with white bow ties sticking out under their thick jackets, one of them lit Helena's face with his flashlight. As she showed her passport and I.D., another man rushed up to her. "Anna," he said softly as he started to embrace her, but she quickly backed away, "No more Anna! Please, all of you. Just Helena now. Please."

They all left for the city.

SIXTEEN

Captain Pryce addressed his small group of men who were now slightly exhausted.

"We won't do any more physical training because I think you've had enough. At least for now. When you have a specific assignment, then we'll see. Cole, I want to know the truth—did your hands hurt, using that rope to pull yourself up to the tower?"

"They were fine, sir."

"I don't want to know about 'fine.' You were putting a lot of pressure on your right hand."

"To tell you the truth, sir, at first my right hand actually hurt more than my left. I was favoring it because I'm right-handed, but when I realized what I was doing I changed and used both hands equally and then it was okay."

"All right. All of you wash up and then we'll take a lunch break."

SEVENTEEN

The elegant Copenhagen Plaza Hotel was across the way from the Tivoli Gardens.

"Helena" took a warm skirt of subdued green and brown colors and a pair of nice, but flat, shoes out of her backpack. After she put them on, she dabbed her lips with very little lipstick and then put her parachute pants and soft boots into the mustard-colored backpack, which she converted to a pretty rose-and-lavender purse by pulling two purse strings. She used the ladies' room at the Copenhagen Plaza Hotel for this quick-change while the men handed their thick jackets to a gentleman who was taking hats and coats. Then the three elegantly dressed men in their tuxedos entered the Library Room, and waited for Helena. The "library" was a relaxed and softly lit room where people could look at the menu, order their food, and then have a drink or two until a waiter came to tell them that their dinner was ready in the dining room.

GENE WILDER

"What will you have to drink, Helena?" Erik Lund said when she joined them. "We were so thirsty that—pardon us—we couldn't wait. So we all got a scotch and soda. Excuse our manners, please."

"I'd love a nice, cold glass of Sancerre if they have it," she said, thinking of Tom and the café and Alfred. Erik signaled to the waiter, who was standing nearby and also dressed in a tuxedo.

"Yes, I heard you, Madam," the waiter said. "And we do have a good bottle of Sancerre." As the waiter was leaving, two German officers came out of the dining room, talking to each other and picking their teeth as they walked by Helena and the three men. They nodded to Helena and the men. *"Guten Abend eine Dame und mehrer Herren."*

The three "friends" of Helena answered in English, "Good evening."

The officer spoke again, this time in English. "Good luck, Mademoiselle, and try not to wear these men out," he said and burst into laughter directed at his partner. Helena didn't smile.

The officer walked up to her. "May I see your papers, please?"

Helena took out her I.D. card and her passport. As the officer looked, he spoke out loud: *"Simonsen . . . dreiundzwanzig jahr alt . . . Katholische."* He looked up and said, "Don't you Catholics ever laugh?"

"I had a dear friend who died yesterday," Helena said. "I'm not always ready for laughing, the way the Jews are."

"I see," said the officer, somewhat awkwardly. "So sorry."

EIGHTEEN

That same evening, Colonel Hartley and Tom sat in the colonel's office having tea.

"I'm told that you're doing very well in your training, but by the look on your face I'd say you disagree."

"By Captain Pryce's perception I'm doing well," Tom said.

"But you don't like him?"

"It's not about liking him, sir, it's just that I don't care for the rules. I work my ass off in training but Captain Pryce won't tell me one word about the woman I love. I had to finagle a way to find out that her name is not Rosenkilde now, it's Simonsen. Helena Simonsen. And I don't know whether she's alive or dead or living in Florida or Siberia or is safe or captured by the Nazis or if she's on our side or theirs. All I know is that it's against the fucking rules to tell me. Pardon my language, sir, but you swore at me once when you visited me in the hospital."

"You're crazy! I don't swear. What did I say?"

"You said, 'I'm from Missouri, so don't fuck around with me.'"

"Oh, yeah. Well, I guess . . . I guess I don't blame you for being angry. Now listen to me . . . I'm going to break the rules. Not even Radar knows the secret life of SOE, so if you tell one living soul I swear I'll break your bloody neck. Understood?"

"Yes, sir."

"I found out that Helena Simonsen got a new passport and was trained in sabotage techniques at a remote Scottish village before being parachuted back into Denmark. That's where she is now, teaching the Danish Resistance how to make bombs in order to blow up trains carrying Nazi soldiers and vital machinery, in and out of Norway. As of yesterday, she's safe. How she is tonight, I don't know."

NINETEEN

"Helena" and her three "friends" stayed for another hour, talking and drinking in the Library Room. Helena thought it was safer to talk about bombs and blowing up trains while they were sitting in an elegant hotel drinking cocktails, assuming it would be improbable for such well-dressed guests to be talking about bombs and trains.

Several officers started leaving the dining room. When Helena saw them she said loudly, "Erik, Mathias, Mads— that's enough about business. I'm tired of talking about bedsheets and pillowcases and female duck feathers— let's talk about music for a change!"

Her three friends shouted, "Bravo, Helena!" and raised their glasses for a toast. A lady sitting having a drink nearby, with a tall blond gentleman, turned her head to look at the woman who was being called Helena. She got up and walked over to Helena's table.

"Anna—"

Anna turned quickly and saw her French teacher, Eva Simonsen. "Please," Anna whispered urgently, "please don't call me Anna. I'm Helena."

"That's not your name. Why are you using my sister's name? You're Anna!"

Anna's three friends stood up. Erik cordially said, "She really is Helena, you know."

"My sister is dead. This is Anna, not Helena," she said loudly.

Helena got up quickly and said very softly, "Eva, I'll tell you why I had to do this if you just wait for a minute." She took Eva's hand. "Please, my dear teacher—just wait for a minute and you'll understand everything."

Anna put her arm around Eva Simonsen's waist and walked her to a corner of the room where there were soft chairs and no people. Anna asked Eva to please sit down. Erik, Mathias, and Mads watched them from their table without being able to hear them.

"Eva, I had to come to Copenhagen and couldn't use my real name or I might have been taken by the Nazis, for sure this time. I knew Helena had died and that she was Catholic, so I used her name to get a passport. Please, dear, please forgive me, but it was terribly important. If they knew I was Anna Rosenkilde they'd know I was Jewish and I'd be in Auschwitz by now." Eva Simonsen stared without talking, but then suddenly put her arms around Anna.

Anna and Eva walked back to Eva's table, where her tall blond companion was waiting. He stood up graciously. "Kai," Eva said, "this is my dear friend Helena, who used to be my pupil. Helena, this is my friend, Kai Brenner."

"Pleasure," he said.

Anna kissed Eva's cheek as she whispered, "Thank you so much, Eva," and then went back to her friends who got their coats and left. The moment they walked outside, Erik Lund said, "I recognized Eva's boyfriend right away—he is a Nazi."

TWENTY

Erik arranged for Helena to stay with his mother that night, since Mrs. Lund lived alone. She lived in a beautiful, almost fairy-tale cottage that rested near a stream that ran down from the Copenhagen Harbor. After watching her husband getting beaten by the Nazis and then dying, along with other people in the factory who refused to stop their slowdown, Mrs. Lund knew exactly what her son was doing now and was proud of him. She greeted "Helena" with open arms that night. She wasn't told about the name "Anna."

Early the next morning, Mrs. Lund served Helena breakfast. "I have tea or coffee . . . whichever you like."

"Coffee, please."

"Good. And do you like rye bread?"

"Very much."

"Good, because I have fresh rye bread with some cheese or jam, and then some Danish pastry. Is that good?"

"Mmm, yes," Helena said.

They sat down together and started eating breakfast. Helena was about to speak when they heard a soft knock on the door. Helena didn't know if she should quickly disappear, but Mrs. Lund said, "It must be Erik," and she got up. But when she opened the door, Eva Simonsen was standing there, next to the tall blond man with whom she'd been at the hotel the night before, but now he was wearing his Nazi uniform. Eva wore an acrid smile. Two Nazi soldiers were standing behind them, just outside the open door. Two other soldiers were standing on each side of a black Mercedes-Benz limousine. All four of the soldiers held their rifles at the ready.

The blond man and Eva Simonsen entered the kitchen, leaving the door wide open.

"I hope we're not disturbing you, Anna," Eva said. "You remember Major Brenner, don't you?"

"I remember his beautiful blond hair," Anna said. "And I also remember my dear friend, Eva. Do you have any idea what might have happened to her?"

"I think some Jews killed my sister, Helena, when all she wanted was to look inside their fishing boat. So now I would like to kill a Jew. You don't mind, do you?"

"I doubt if it happened that way to Helena, but you wouldn't believe me anyway," Anna said.

"No, I wouldn't. Good morning, Mrs. Lund. How nice to see you."

"Anna, come with us right now," Major Brenner said.

"Yes, I'll come. No violence, please. May I say good-bye to Mrs. Lund, who knows nothing of the things we've been talking about?"

"Go ahead," he said as he moved closer to her.

Anna embraced Mrs. Lund, kissed her and then spoke in Danish: *"Farvel kaere frue . . . tak for alt."* (Good-bye, dear . . . thank you for everything.)

"You didn't even eat much of your breakfast," Mrs. Lund said.

"May I wear my jacket, Major? I think it's rather cold today," Anna said.

"Where is it?" Major Brenner asked.

"Just over that chair."

"I'll get it," the major said as he went to the chair and took Anna's jacket. "Now we go," he said as he took hold of Anna's arm and walked her to the doorway.

When Eva, Anna, and Major Brenner walked out of the house the major saw that one of his soldiers was kneeling on the side of the Mercedes-Benz. *"Was zum Teufel machst du da?"* (What the hell are you doing there?)

"Reifenpanne. Ich werde es sofort beheben, Herr Major." (Flat tire, sir. I'll fix it quickly, Major.)

Submachine guns suddenly blasted Eva, Major Brenner, and the four Nazi soldiers. Erik, Mathias, and Mads came rushing out from behind separate bushes. Erik knelt down quickly to feel the pulses. "Dead!" he said with a smile. Then he got up and looked at Anna.

"Hello, there! I thought that rotten Nazi might do something like this," Erik shouted as he began taking off Major Brenner's uniform.

"How nice to see the three of you again," Anna said. "Erik, what are you doing with him?"

"I'm taking all of the uniforms from these swine; they might come in handy one day. Then we dump their naked bodies into the Copenhagen Harbor for a nice, cold swim. I even told young Mathias here that he has to be a gentleman and not look at the dead lady when she's naked, so now he's fixing the flat tire that he stuck his knife into."

Mrs. Lund came out of the house with a smile on her face. "I knew my son would save you," she said. "I *knew* it. Now come into the house Anna, or Helena, or whatever name you want, and eat your breakfast. I made that Danish pastry especially for you."

"Hey, Mama Lund!" Erik hollered. "When we come back would you also make a little breakfast for Mathias and Mads and your son, Erik, if you happen to remember me? We are also cold and hungry."

TWENTY-ONE

Tom and the three men who were in training with him sat in Captain Pryce's office repeating their fake German and French names.

"Cole, I'm told you speak French."

"Yes, sir," Tom answered.

"How well?" Captain Pryce asked.

"*Je ne veux pas vous insulter, mais je parle français aussi bien que vous parlez anglais,* sir."

"Hmm. I think I was just insulted, but in this case I'm glad. Where did you learn it?"

"My mother was French."

"I see. The rest of you fellows can go home now. I want to talk to Lieutenant Cole alone for awhile."

The three other men picked up their jackets and headed for the door. Alex, the fellow with whom Tom was closest, whispered "Good luck, old bean," as he passed Tom.

Captain Pryce and Tom were alone in the old manor house and the wood fire was still burning in the fireplace.

"Would you like some tea, Cole, or would you prefer something a little stronger?"

"Tea would be fine, sir. I'm guessing I'd better have a clear head for whatever you're about to tell me."

Captain Pryce picked up the phone. "Terry, would you please bring us one tea and one double brandy." Then he turned back to Tom. "You've resented my holding back information from you for quite awhile," Pryce said.

"Only because I didn't care for the rules, sir."

"I'll tell you now what I wasn't allowed to say before. Anna Rosenkilde was able to get out of Denmark and go to Sweden, with a little help from her Danish friends. I couldn't use her real name before."

"Thank you, sir."

"Wait, before thanking me. Have you heard of a group called the Maquis?"

"No, I haven't."

"It comes from a word that means 'bushes that grow along country roads.'"

"Sounds nice," Tom said.

"Several of the French POWs escaped from prison and joined the Maquis, which distinguished itself by committing atrocities against German soldiers. They hid in the bushes and darted out to kidnap officers and then executed them."

"I'm not crying," Tom said.

"Up till now four female SOE agents were executed at

Dachau. Four of our other women agents were captured and taken to a concentration camp in France, known as Natzweiler."

Tom's heart began beating faster as Corporal Johnson entered the room with a tray holding the tea service and a small glass of brandy. "Here you are, sir," he said as he placed the tray on the table next to Pryce.

"Here's your tea, Lieutenant."

"No thank you, sir. I'm trying to wait patiently."

Pryce took a deep swig of his brandy, then looked at Tom. "Most of these women aided the escape of downed Allied airmen and Jews. Are you sure you wouldn't like a shot of brandy, Cole?"

"I'm sure, sir. Please go on."

"There was one French woman, by the name of Madame Lauro, who poured hydrochloric acid and nitric acid on German food supplies in freight cars that were running on French railroads. Anna worked with her in France for two weeks and idolized her. Madame Lauro was just captured and sent to Natzweiler. When Anna was in Sweden she found this out and asked the head of SOE, by radio, for permission to be sent to Alsace to help Madame Lauro escape before they sent her to a camp in Germany."

As he listened, Tom stared out of a window, watching a house martin that kept flying back and forth to feed its newborns.

"Would you tell me what you're thinking, Tom?"

"Where is Natzweiler?"

"It's in Alsace-Lorraine, which is in France, but it's on the border of Germany."

"Would you send me there? Please."

"I don't have the authority to do that. I can pass your request on to the top if you wish."

"I do wish, sir."

TWENTY-TWO

Maj. Gen. Colin Gubbins was the director of the SOE. Colonel Hartley was the general's chief of staff and Captain Pryce was the colonel's training officer. They all sat in Colonel Hartley's office, along with Tom, who sat in a straight-backed chair listening to Major General Gubbins who was looking straight at Tom, as the scents of tea, half-eaten biscuits, and cigarette smoke filled the air.

"Our agent in Alsace, Brian Lewis, radioed me yesterday. I'm going to tell you what he told me:

"First of all, he said that four women entered Natzweiler, escorted by SS officers. The first woman was of middle height, maybe twenty-three or four, with a gray bow in her short blonde hair.

"He thought the second woman was a little older and taller than the first woman, maybe Jewish. She wore a black coat and had very dark hair.

"The third woman also had dark hair, maybe twenty-eight. She carried a ratty fur coat and wore a flannel suit. Brian thought she was obviously English and looked like she had been in jail. Just a guess, he said. The others wore lipstick, she didn't.

"He said the fourth woman was tall, he thought she was maybe thirty and—get a load of this—she was wearing an elegant dress.

"Now my guess is that Diana Rowden was the third woman, the one who looked English. Actually, her mother was Jewish. As far as that second woman, who Brian thought looked Jewish, well she was. I'm sure it was Yolanda Beekman. Her father was a Russian Jew I met in Brussels in 1939. When Germany invaded France, Yolanda joined the French Resistance and spent most of her time carrying messages for us between our agents in France. As for the first and fourth women, I haven't got a clue. What do you think, Pryce?"

"I would guess that the fourth woman is Madame Lauro."

"Tell me why," the general said.

"Well, we have no idea what she looks like, sir. All we know is that she poured acid on German soldiers' food supplies in freight trains that were running on French railroads. She always worked alone and at night. Then she gets captured and is sent to Natzweiler wearing an elegant dress while an SS man escorts her in. I'd say she must be a strong French woman who is proud to wear her elegant dress to prison, a little like spitting in the Nazis' eyes. I think only a French woman would do that."

"Tom?" Colonel Hartley asked.

"I agree with Captain Pryce, that the fourth woman is Madame Lauro. Does Natzweiler have a crematorium, sir?"

"Pryce?" the colonel asked.

"They do have a crematorium now. A few weeks ago Brian told me that there used to be a small hotel about a mile above the concentration camp—probably for skiers—but it was reconstructed into a small gas chamber. That was recently, sir."

"So what are you getting at, Cole?" the general asked.

"Do you know if Madame Lauro is Jewish, sir?" Tom asked.

"Let's say that she is," the general said.

"Well if she *is* Jewish, why didn't they send Yolanda Beekman, Diana Rowden, and Madame Lauro to Dachau? They send most Jews to Auschwitz or Dachau. Why send them to Natzweiler, which is near the top of a mountain?"

"Why do you think?" the general asked.

"I think because of the gas chamber. But it seems crazy, because if they wanted to kill them, why there? I also think that the first woman you mentioned—the short blonde with a gray bow in her hair—is Anna Rosenkilde."

"Anna has long auburn hair," Captain Pryce corrected him.

"I think she cut it short and dyed it," Tom said.

"Why?" Captain Pryce said.

"She didn't want to be identified as Rosenkilde, the Jew," Tom answered quickly. "So she cut her hair and dyed it. Each time I was with her she wore a pink bow. After it got smudged and dirty she probably kept it in her pocket, but she, too, is a very proud woman. I think she wanted to have that bow in her hair in the same way that Madame Lauro wore an elegant dress when they were escorted by the SS. As you told me, Captain Pryce, Anna adored Madame Lauro, after working with her in France, and wanted to help her escape. I know that Anna is Jewish. That makes four Jews and a gas chamber in Natzweiler."

There was a long silence as the general and the colonel looked at each other.

"Are you suggesting something, Lieutenant, or just showing us how smart you are?" the general asked.

"Send me to Natzweiler, now, before it's too late."

"Do you realize what you're asking?"

"I do," Tom answered.

"Are you really so brave, Lieutenant Cole?" the general asked.

"No, sir, but I am very smart, and I speak German and French fluently, and I believe I would be as good as anyone you can find."

"What would you need?" the general asked.

"An authentic SS uniform, pants, gloves, socks, shoes,

and a Luger. I would need an authentic French farmer's outfit, and I would need a radio operator who knew how to use a submachine gun, and I would need two French Resistance fighters in Alsace who would wear authentic Nazi uniforms and who would also have submachine guns."

"How the hell do you know all this?" the general asked.

"Because I was a bloody medic in Bastogne. *Very* bloody."

The general looked at Colonel Hartley. Colonel Hartley nodded his head "yes" with a tiny smile.

TWENTY-THREE

Tom sat as calmly as he could as the RAF Lysander plane flew him to Alsace. His radio operator sat across from him.

"ABOUT THREE MINUTES, LIEUTENANT," the copilot called out from the open cockpit door. Tom nodded. His heart rushed when he heard how close they were. He had gone over all the plans several times with Captain Pryce and now he sat in a plane going to the French/German border. He remembered hearing Colonel Hartley saying, "Eventually you'll be judged by your ability to make decisions on your own."

He remembered the pink bow Anna was wearing in her hair on the night they met. He remembered her giggle very clearly, and her jokes, and how she suddenly reached for his hand when the alarm sounded. Or did *he* reach for *her* hand when he saw how frightened she was? Most of all he remembered the single night they made love in her room.

He looked across at his radio operator, Jamie Clark,

who gave him a confident smile and a little thumbs-up sign.

Tom took a deep breath and let it out slowly. He looked down at his backpack, stuffed with his French clothes, an SS uniform, and several hand grenades. His German MP40 submachine gun was strapped around his shoulder.

"ONE MINUTE," the copilot called out. Tom pictured Anna again. *Remember that her hair is short and blonde now. Don't go to pieces if she's dead. . . .*

AT THREE hundred feet, Tom and Jamie Clark jumped into the darkness, following the parachuted equipment that they had just sent ahead of them. They landed safely on a somewhat level field that was drawn out for them by the army architect who knew this territory. They were now forty meters above the red-stoned quarry that Hitler used for rebuilding Nuremberg until he ran out of money. They were a half mile from the concentration camp. Tom and Jamie quickly buried their parachutes in the nearby woods. After setting up their small portable tent they climbed in.

Jamie set up his wireless and sent the short message: "Everybody's rockin.' Everybody's rockin.'" When he got the confirmation, he packed up his radio. "So far, so good," he said. "Are you all right, sir?"

"Just a little worried about posing as an SS shit."

"I heard you practicing on the plane, sir. You'll be fine."

"I hope you're right."

"I don't think I told you that I met your lady friend when she needed a little help with her wireless radio," Jamie said. "She's a very sweet girl."

"If she's still alive. When are the Resistance fellows supposed to be here?"

"They said eight a.m. Why don't you try to get some sleep, sir?"

"Jamie, you'd better stop calling me 'sir' or 'Lieutenant.' From now on my name is Gerhard Lange, but when we enter the concentration camp I am Herr Standarten-führer Lange. Clear?"

"Yes, sir. I mean, *Jawohl Herr Standhat, Herr Stan*—oh shit! Sorry sir. No, I mean, *Jawohl Herr Stan-dar-ten-führer Lange*," Jamie said.

"You'd better practice a little more in the morning, Jamie. For now let's get some sleep."

TWENTY-FOUR

The sun came up slowly. It was 6:15 a.m. After feeling his face Tom said, "If you don't mind, Jamie, would you give me a shave? Right now I don't trust myself with a razor on my face, and I don't want to look like I've got a hangover."

"Did you sleep at all?" Jamie asked.

"No, but I'm all right, just a little nervous."

Jamie put a glob of shaving cream on Tom's face. "Let it sink in for a while to soften your whiskers. I've laid out your uniform. Let's go outside so I can see your face better."

When they both crawled out of the tent, they saw that they were perched on a small mountain surrounded by a forest of evergreens. Tom gazed at it all for a few seconds while he stretched his legs. "A concentration camp on a mountain with a beautiful forest . . . it's an oxymoron," he said.

"If you're an SS Standartenführer—whatever the hell that means—what am *I* supposed to be?" Jamie asked as he started shaving Tom.

"It means that I'm the assistant to Heinrich Himmler and you're the assistant to me. I've also just made you my barber, but I'm afraid there's no extra pay, Jamie. I'll make it up to you if we get back to London."

"We *will* get back. I promise," Jamie said. "But why are you the Führer?"

"I'm not *the Führer*! Jesus, Jamie. I'm only *a führer*. Just means I'm a leader. And if I'm Heinrich Himmler's assistant, I must be damned important. I'm counting on that because I want to scare the shit out of those Nazis when I walk in."

After Jamie finished shaving Tom, he helped Tom on with his field-gray SS uniform. The lightning bolt double S shape was embroidered on the collar of his uniform and his shoulder pads denoted that the uniform belonged to a colonel. Every aspect of the rest of his uniform— boots, socks, hat, belt, and Luger pistol—had all been taken from dead SS officers and then stored in London.

"Well," Tom asked as he stood still, as if he were a model in a fashion show, "do I really look like an authentic Nazi bastard?"

"You certainly do, Herr Standartenführer Lange," Jamie said.

"Good for you. You'd better get into your corporal's uniform. And Jamie—if you ever hear me say, 'Tuez les tous,' it means 'Shoot them all.'"

"Tuez les tous," Jamie repeated.

"Yes. Remember that."

AT 8:00 A.M., a long, black Mercedes drove up the hill, with stolen identifying command flags on its fenders. It stopped next to Tom and Jamie. Two men in gray, Nazi uniforms got out of the car and walked up to Tom.

"Heil Hitler, Monsieur," the taller man said with a smile as he gave a Nazi salute. "My name it is Claude Breton and here is my partner, Gilles Piccard." The two Frenchmen shook hands with Tom.

"This is my radio man, Jamie Clark," Tom said. Jamie shook hands with both of them. Claude Breton turned to his partner and said, *"Il ressemble a un porc SS très bonne, tu ne trouves pas?"*

"I hope I do resemble an SS swine, *et vous les regardez comme des bon nazis,"* Tom replied.

"Ah, you speak the good French. I hope your German is just as good," Claude said.

"Mon allemand est très bon, probablement meilleur que votre anglais," Tom answered.

"Bravo! So . . . are you both ready for the grand entrance?"

"We are," Tom said.

"Good. We have shined your Mercedes very nice I hope, Herr Standartenführer Lange."

"Sehr gut," Tom said. "And now, let's *schnell gehen.*"

Tom sat in the backseat of the shiny Mercedes. Jamie sat next to him as his "German assistant." He had his German submachine gun at his side. Claude drove and Gilles sat next to him in the front seat, both looking quite official. They also had Luger pistols at their sides and submachine guns on the floor.

Claude drove the Mercedes slowly down the hill.

"Why on earth did they build a gas chamber if they already had a crematorium?" Tom asked as they drove slowly toward Natzweiler.

"For the Jews," Gilles Piccard answered.

"Are you making a joke?" Tom asked.

"I am Jewish, Monsieur. I don't make those kinds of jokes."

"I'm sorry," Tom said.

"Men and women Jews are now sent from Auschwitz to Natzweiler to get murdered in the gas chamber. And when their bodies are still warm they are sent to the University Hospital in Strasbourg for research by a Nazi doctor named August Hirt."

"But they're already dead," Tom said.

"How do you say mishuganah in English?" Gilles asked.

"Mishuganah," Tom answered.

"The mishuganah doctor wants to expand the skulls

79

and skeletons of Jews to prove that they're really animals. He considers it important to hurry because he believes the Jewish population will be exterminated soon and that Jewish skeletons will be as rare as dinosaurs."

"He's insane," Tom said.

"So is Hitler," Gilles said.

TWENTY-FIVE

A heavy mist hovered over the concentration camp. "This cloudiness might be good for us," Tom said softly as the Mercedes approached the gate. "Please don't any of you try to speak in German unless you absolutely have to. Just 'Ja' or 'Nein.'"

Josef Kramer, the bulbous commandant of Natzweiler, stood lazily at attention when our car pulled to a stop. Claude and Gilles got out and stood on each side of it, holding their submachine guns as Tom stepped out of the car. Jamie quickly got out, with his submachine gun, and stood next to Tom.

"I am Hauptsturmführer, Josef Kramer, commandant of Natzweiler," he said while giving a lazy *sieg heil*. "And who exactly are you?" he asked in German.

"Stand up straight you bloated pig, and give a real '*Sieg Heil*'!" Tom said in German. "I am SS Standartenführer Gerhard Lange. *Colonel* Lange, in case you're so blind, *Captain* Kramer, that you can't see my shoulder pads?"

"I . . . I am . . . so sorry, Herr Oberst. Please forgive me. What can I do for you, sir?"

"Open the fucking gate. I want to see the four Jews who arrived recently."

"Open the gate!" the commandant shouted to a guard in the small tower above the gate. As the gate slowly opened Captain Kramer said, "But there are only three Jews, Herr Oberst. We discovered that the other woman is a Catholic."

"Did she have short blonde hair and answer to the name of Helena Simonsen?"

"Why, yes. That's right."

"That woman is not Catholic, she is a Jew! You read a fake passport. Her real name is Anna Rosenkilde and we've been searching for her for the past two weeks. When do you put these Jews in the gas chamber?"

"This evening, sir, when the sun starts to go down. That's when the male prisoners are eating and . . . we don't like them to see the women leave the camp, because they will know where they are going."

"Then I must see these women now! All of them. Are they together in one cell?"

"Yes, Herr Oberst."

"Do you have a single cell?"

"I do, sir.

"Then put the Rosenkilde woman in the single cell.

She's the one I suspect the most. DO IT NOW! I'll see the other Jews after I talk with her."

"Of course, Herr Oberst," the commandant said as he ran off to the prison. Gilles nudged Claude and whispered, *"Notre amie est brillant."*

TWENTY-SIX

Tom and his "guards" followed Commandant Kramer into the prison.

"Just here, on your left, is the single cell." He opened the cell door and then hurried away shouting, "I return immediately, Herr Oberst, with the Rosenkilde woman."

Tom went inside the minuscule cell and lowered his hat over his right eye. "Jamie," Tom said, "stand near the entrance to the prison but turn away, toward the camp yard. Anna might recognize you as she passes by you. Gilles and Claude, stand outside this cell, against the wall, and look out for any Gestapo who come this way, especially if they're running. But *don't shoot* unless they raise their weapons."

Tom could hear the heavy footsteps of Commandant Kramer rushing back along the dark prison corridor. Behind his shadow Tom could make out Anna's smaller one.

"Here, Standartenführer Lange. Here she is," the commandant yelled with sweat streaming down his fat face as he shoved Anna into the cell with Tom.

"Good! Now leave and do not come back till I call," Tom said in a husky German whisper.

"Yes, Herr Oberst. I understand," the commandant said, trying to match Tom's whisper as he hurried away.

Tom began to tremble when he looked at Anna. Her soft, white skin was bruised and dirty, and her raspberry cheeks were red with bloodstains. He wanted to come closer to her, to hold her, but he was afraid that she might scream. Anna didn't look at him. Her small bow was still in her hair, but it was hardly pink anymore.

What a brave woman, he thought. *How could I have suspected that she might have been a double agent?*

"Are you hungry?" Tom asked.

"Not in the least," Anna answered quickly, without turning her head toward him.

"Even if I could offer you some sautéed octopus from the Shepherdess Café?" he asked.

Her eyes popped open wide. When she turned to look at him she was about scream with happiness, but Tom put his hand over her mouth. "You must be very quiet now, Anna," Tom said softly as he took off his hat and then kissed her. When she looked at his face she could hardly catch her breath.

"Tom—" she tried to say without choking, but then she suddenly pulled away when she saw Claude and Gilles standing against the wall in their German uniforms. Tom said, "Those are our friends, Anna, from the French Resistance. And Jamie Clark is guarding the door. He helped you once with your wireless radio, remember?" When Gilles touched two fingers to his lips and threw a kiss to Anna, she buried her face in Tom's chest.

"Anna, lead me to the cell with the three other women, but you must look cold, the way you did when the commandant brought you to me," Tom said. "Your tears are all right, it will just look as if I said frightening things to you. Whatever happens in the next few minutes, you mustn't smile. Understand?"

Anna nodded, "yes."

"Now step out of this cell with me and walk slowly by my side. Our friends will be in front and behind us. Can you do this?"

Anna again nodded, "yes," and they walked out of the cell. As they came close to Claude and Gilles, Tom said, "Both of you walk in front of us, not too fast, just a steady walk. Clear?"

"Ja," they both said.

When they passed Jamie, he smiled at Anna. "Don't do that!" Tom said. "You don't know her and you don't like her."

"Sorry. It won't happen again," Jamie said.

"Walk a few feet behind us, Jamie. If you see any black-shirted guards don't rush to conclusions, and don't nod to them, even if they nod to you. Just be ready with your submachine gun and remember my French signal."

When they reached the unlocked cell that held the three other women, Tom walked in with Anna. The three women looked bitter and defiant until they saw Anna take Tom's hand, which baffled them.

"I'm not an SS officer," Tom said quietly. "I'm in the SOE and we're going to try to get you out of this place. Those three men standing outside are not Germans. Two of them are French Resistance and the other is my radio operator, also in the SOE." Yolanda Beekman and Madame Lauro closed their eyes and smiled. Diana Rowden took Anna's hand and held on to it.

"I have to ask each of you to do something special . . . don't smile or show any happiness until we're out of here. Let the Nazis see your bitterness. If you want to spit on someone, spit on me. They'd believe that. It's probably happened to most of them often enough. You are four remarkable women, and I'm proud to know you. Now I'm going to get the commandant."

As Tom stepped out of the cell, he saw Commandant Kramer walking toward him, confidently this time, along with four black-shirted soldiers.

"So, Oberst Lange, or should I say SS Standartenführer Lange, assistant to Heinrich Himmler. I want you to meet four very good friends of mine," Captain Kramer said. "They are Waffen-SS soldiers, extremely loyal to Hitler, and would die for him without a second's hesitation."

"Commandant Kramer," Tom said, "may I ask why you pay me this unexpected pleasure right now, when I'm in the middle of an interrogation?"

"Of course you may ask. It's because I called Reichsführer Himmler's main office and was told that they had no record of a colonel named Gerhard Lange," Kramer said with a slow and caustic smile.

Tom looked at the eyes of the four Waffen-SS soldiers whose hands rested near the triggers on their guns.

"May I ask you one more question, Captain?"

"Of course you may."

"Did you speak with Himmler himself, or did you get this brilliant information from some asshole who works in his office?"

"I—I spoke with SS Sturmbannführer Rudolph Brandt. Major Brandt told me himself that—"

"You idiot!" Tom screamed. "I work for Heinrich Himmler, not Major Brandt! I shall recommend your extraordinary stupidity to Himmler himself."

By their faces Tom could see that the Waffen-SS soldiers weren't sure of what to do. The women in the prison cell thought they understood what Tom was doing, even though they didn't understand German very well, but they were terribly frightened of what would happen if it didn't work.

Claude, Gilles, and Jamie had no idea what they were saying, but they could tell that it wasn't good.

Tom said, "Let's calm down, please. All of us. Perhaps I'm overreacting to Commandant Kramer's stupid mistake. I am not used to being questioned about my rank and the job that Reichsfürer Himmler gave to me personally. Will you please forgive me, Commandant?"

"Why . . . yes," the commandant said hesitantly. "Of course, Oberst Lange."

Tom turned to Claude and Gilles. "Pas le commandant, mais tuez les autre," he said very calmly.

Claude and Gilles blasted their submachine guns and slaughtered the four SS black shirts. Commandant Kramer was so frightened he bent over, as if he were peeing in his pants, which he probably was. Claude and Gilles checked to see if the Waffen-SS soldiers were dead. They were.

"I like your style, Monsieur," Claude said.

"And I like your French," Gilles said.

"And now, Commandant Kramer, you have a choice: Walk with us, all of us, without crying or signaling to the camp guards or making any strange movements—and you live. I promise. If not, you're going to die. For sure."

"I want to live," Commandant Kramer said with two tears running down his cheeks.

"You're sure?"

"Yes, I swear to you."

"All right. I want you to put your hand around my left arm, as if we've become friends. I hope we're far enough away that the guards couldn't hear the shooting, but I don't know. So let's walk briskly, but not too fast. And ladies, try to look lifeless, like you're going to the gas chamber," Tom said.

As they they left the prison and walked across the camp grounds toward the gate, they saw that the camp guards were watching their commandant holding Tom's arm. "*Sie sehen gut aus zusammen* ("They look cute together.), one of them said. Another guard said, "*Ja, vielleicht werden sie heiraten*" ("Maybe they'll get married."). Most of them smiled as the women passed by. The guards knew that the women were heading for the gas chamber. Some of them whistled at the ladies. When Madame Lauro spit in Tom's face, all the guards laughed. A big guard said, "*Ich hatte gerne, dass die Dicke ihren mantel und ihre kleider aussieht und mir zeigt, was sie zu bieten hat.*" ("I'd like to watch that big one take off her coat and her clothes and let me see what she's got.") As they approached the gate, Tom told the commandant to tell the guard at the top of the small tower to open the gate.

"Open the gate," the commandant hollered to the guard.

The guard looked down at Claude and Gilles and the women.

"Open it, open it," the commandant hollered. "Are you deaf?"

"No, sir. Sorry sir," he said as his face turned red. He began turning the wheel that opened the gate.

"You're coming with us, Commandant," Tom said.

"But . . . no, you said . . ."

"I will keep my promise, I'm not going to kill you, but you're coming with us. Tell your man at the gate that you will be at the gas chamber for the next hour."

"I'll be at the gas chamber for about an hour," the commandant barked to the guard.

"Yes, sir," the guard shouted back.

When the gate was open, they all walked out and climbed into the Mercedes. Claude drove with their prisoner next to him and Tom on his other side. Tom squeezed Anna's hand as she sidled into the seat behind them with the other women. Gilles and Jamie sat on the small seat behind the women. As they drove away, Claude asked in French, "Are we really going to the gas chamber?"

"No," Tom answered in French. "I'm sure they'll be looking for us there in a very short while. We're going to Strasbourg."

"You were smart, my friend," Claude said in French. "With a little luck we can get to our destination before they know where we are."

Claude turned off the road that would have led them to the gas chamber and pulled onto the Reichsautobahn that led to Strasbourg. "I think it would be safer to drive a little more slowly," Tom said. Claude drove at a moderate speed. The women relaxed just a little, but as every truck that passed was filled with German soldiers, they couldn't help wondering if they might be stopped at any moment.

TWENTY-SEVEN

When they arrived on the outskirts of Strasbourg, Claude asked Tom, in French, "Where are we going?"

"To the University Hospital," Tom answered.

"Oh . . . to see my doctor friend?"

"Yes."

"It will be a lovely surprise for him."

"I hope so." Tom then called out to Gilles.

"Yes, Monsieur?" Gilles called back.

Tom said, in French, "Would you please ask one of the ladies if she would be kind enough to cut two strips of her white petticoat: one to fit around a man's head and another to tie his hands?"

"A heavy man's head?" Gilles said with a smile.

"Yes."

Madame Lauro poked Gilles. "I heard what he said. Do you have a knife, Monsieur?"

Gilles pulled out his knife and handed it to her. "Be careful, Madame. It's very sharp," he said.

"I'm very good with sharp knives, Monsieur. I've used them many, many times." Then Madame Lauro lifted the skirt of her elegant dress and started cutting her petticoat. "I think I understand the purpose of ruining my petticoat. I'm very proud." When she was finished, she handed the two strips of petticoat to Tom. "Use it in good health, Monsieur, as we say in both Jewish and French."

When they arrived they saw that the University Hospital was huge, very white, and extraordinarily clean, with no students or doctors going in and out.

"Madame Lauro, would you please hold the commandant's head firmly, so that he can't see what I'm doing?" Tom said in French.

"With pleasure, Monsieur."

Tom took out a pen from his jacket—a German pen—and began writing on one of the strips of petticoat, in German:

Doctor August Hirt—I am Jewish

Then Tom took off the commandant's military jacket and his pants as Commandant Kramer screamed hysterically, "What are you doing? You said you weren't going to kill me. You promised."

In German Tom said, "I am not going to kill you, Commandant Kramer. But I don't want you to see where we're going, or running to a policeman. They'll take care

93

of you in the hospital, I promise." Then he wrapped the strip of petticoat with the writing around the commandant's head, tightly, and then tied the commandant's hands behind him. "Now, let's get you out of the car, Commandant."

Tom placed the commandant on the hospital steps. "There are just three steps up and then the door to go inside. I'm sure you can manage this, Commandant Kramer. Just go slowly."

When Tom got back to the Mercedes, everyone applauded. Anna was sitting in the front seat. "Is it all right Tom? They all told me that we could applaud now," she said.

"They were right," Tom said. "Thank you all. But now let's get the hell out of here."

TWENTY-EIGHT

"Where do we go now?" Madame Lauro asked.

"Now we go to the home of my father," Gilles said. "He was Italian Jew, but when Mussolini and Hitler become pals, my father gets the hell out fast and goes to Alsace. He met a beautiful girl, who is French, and she becomes my mama, and they have a beautiful baby boy, who is me."

"I think he exaggerates a little," Claude said.

"So what's his name?" Madame Lauro asked.

"My father can't keep his Italian name, which was too Jewish for the Nazis, so he uses his wife's name: Piccard. And when I marry a beautiful Jewish woman we get another Piccard, my little boy, Didi. The Nazis think we are a very good Catholic family. If the Germans ever try to fool my little Didi with trick questions, my papa taught him to say, in Italian, 'I am just a little boy and speak only Italiano.' But that's the only Italian Didi knows."

* * *

THEY REACHED the outskirts of Strasbourg, close to the French/German border, and rode through a lovely neighborhood in Alsace where the houses had flower boxes in the windows and a river that kept traveling alongside them. Claude stopped in front of a cottage on the edge of a forest and Gilles turned to his audience: "Voilà! Here is my home. Will you please come in and meet my family? Then Claude and I will find a good spot to hide this shiny Mercedes before the Nazis see it. By the way, Claude is not Jewish. He is a good Catholic and we go hunting together almost every day . . . for Nazis."

Gilles jumped out of the car and knocked on the front door. Tom and Jamie emptied their backpacks and wireless radio from the trunk and then helped the four women out of the car. Claude, Gilles, and Jamie kept their weapons with them.

When the door opened, an older woman, a younger woman, and a little boy popped out. Gilles hugged and kissed each of them, then turned to Tom, Jamie, and the ladies: "Here is my mama, Isabelle; my wife, Amalie; and my little boy, Didi. Please come say hello, get a hug from Mama, go to the bathroom, wash up, anything you like. Where is Papa?"

"Papa is here!" a handsome man with silver hair said as he came out of the house. "This is my former Italian papa," Gilles said. "Now he is the well-known Frenchman, Emile Piccard." Gilles hugged his father. Then Emile Piccard said hello to each of his guests in turn.

"Claude and I will return fast, Papa," Gilles shouted as he got into the Mercedes.

"You got to go faster than that!" his father shouted.

"Why?" Gilles shouted.

"Oh, mio Dio! Gilles—when the sun goes down today IT'S PASSOVER."

TWENTY-NINE

Three of the ladies took a shower, and what a relief it was. Anna shampooed her hair with a shampoo bar she found near the soap bar. She also scrubbed her pink bow, knowing how pretty Tom thought it looked on her auburn hair. He had told her that her dirty, gray bow was how he had realized that the woman with short blonde hair was her.

Diana Rowden, the thin English woman, was more modest than the others and didn't want to remove all of her clothes. She chose to clean herself from the wash basin. Yolanda Beekman and Madame Lauro stayed under the shower for as long as they could until they were told that the Passover service was about to begin.

Tom and Jamie wore the authentic French clothes that the SOE had given them for the time when they wouldn't have to be in German uniforms. After Tom shaved, he looked like a clean-cut farmer.

Claude, Gilles, and Jamie kept their submachine guns at their sides.

WHEN EVERYONE had been seated, Papa Emile said: "Who is the youngest person among us?"

"Me!" his grandson said quickly.

"You're sure you are the youngest, Didi?"

"I am only four years old."

"Okay, then you're the youngest. Are you ready to ask the four questions?"

"I fink so."

"You *fink* so? You *fink* you can ask the questions in French?"

"Oui!" Didi answered.

"Allons vite."

"Pourquoi cette nuit . . . c'est différent que tous des autres nuits?"

A loud knock on the door interrupted Didi and startled everyone. Before the next knock could come a German officer barged in quickly. As he entered the room, his sergeant stood in the doorway with a submachine gun in his hands.

"Good evening, ladies and gentlemen," the officer said. "I'm Captain Erhard Heiden. Are we having a nice time tonight?"

"It was nice until you came in so quickly," Grandpa said.

"I'm so sorry. Do we have a little celebration here?"

"Yes," Grandpa said.

"And is Passover the special occasion?"

"No, it's to celebrate my grandson's birthday. He is now four years old."

"Oh, how wonderful," the officer said as he walked over to Didi. "Hello, young man. Congratulations. You are a cute little boy. Can you say hello to me?"

Didi looked at grandpa, who nodded okay, so Didi said, "I am just a little boy and I speak only Italian."

"But you just spoke in English," the officer said.

"No, I mean, *sono un ragazzino e parla solo italiano,*" Didi said quickly.

"How nice," the officer said. "May I see your penis, please?"

Grandpa stood up. "Why do you say such things to my grandson?"

"Because, Herr Piccard, I want to see if he has been circumcised, like a good little Jewish boy."

Tom stayed seated and said calmly, *"Und warum frangst du nicht alle von uns, ihnen unsere penis?"* (And why don't you ask each of us to show our penis?)

"Your German is excellent," the officer replied. "Do you also speak French?"

"Just a little," Tom said as he looked at Jamie, Claude, and Gilles. "Let me see if I can still remember my French . . . Tuez les tout."

Claude blasted his machine gun at the sergeant while Gilles and Jamie, without even glancing at each other to coordinate their movement, slaughtered the German officer. Didi ran into his grandfather's arms, frightened, but he didn't cry.

"This is not exactly the Passover I imagined," Grandpa said. Then he lifted Elijah's wine cup. "To Elijah, who we hope will come soon to announce when all people will be free. Amen. And now, if you don't mind, let's pass over the rest of the Passover and eat the chickens that my beautiful wife, Isabelle, has made for this occasion. Gilles!"

"Yes, Papa?"

"Before you bury those two swine, would you please pour us all a little French wine? No! A *lot* of French wine."

THIRTY

The four ladies stood outside, getting hugs from Gilles's mother, Isabelle, and his wife, Amalie. Isabelle had sweaters and jackets that she was handing out to the other women.

"Don't argue with me, please," she said. "We've got plenty of sweaters and coats that Gilles gets from God knows where. We don't want you catching a cold while you're waiting for the plane. If it doesn't land, you could freeze to death. Now get in the car."

The ladies each accepted a last-minute hug from Grandpa and then got into the Mercedes. Didi waved good-bye as the car drove off using only its parking lights. Five minutes later they had entered the forest.

"Everything on time?" Tom asked Jamie, who sat in the front seat with the wireless radio on his lap.

"Still twenty-two hundred hours, Tom, if everything stays on schedule," Jamie said.

"It all seems too good to be true," Madame Lauro

said. "We're in the middle of a forest and they're sending an airplane for us? It seems like a fantasy," she said with a laugh.

"But won't the Nazis see the lights?" Diana Rowden asked.

"The 161 Lysander only flies into enemy territory on moonlit nights. It's a quiet plane and sneaky, and all it needs is the length of a football field to land and take off," Jamie said to Miss Rowden and all the other women. "Our pilot, Chris, has landed on this field many, many times, and I've been with him. The moon is bright tonight or else we wouldn't be here, so don't worry."

"One more mile," Claude said.

In a few minutes they reached what had once been a soccer field. The French Resistance had kept the earth clear of branches and bottles on a regular basis. The Mercedes stopped and Claude turned off the motor. After the engine sighed into silence, all the women spoke about what each of them wanted to do when they arrived in London. Madame Lauro and Yolanda had never been there before but had read about London and seen photos.

Anna was wonderfully excited. She held Tom's hand and kissed it several times. She kept thanking him for rescuing her and the other women. "Will you take me out two or three or fifty times when we get back, and can we go to the Shepherdess Café and order all the food and wine that they won't have again?"

"Absolutely," Tom said.

"Do you promise?"

"I promise, if you don't ever tell me that your job is to send radio waves to the sky. You don't know what you put me through when Bertie said she didn't know you."

"I'm so sorry, Tom. I wasn't allowed to tell anyone what my real job was, not even someone I loved. Do you forgive me? Tell me that you forgive me."

"Yes I do. I do, so calm down and let's try to see the pilot's signal."

Everyone looked at the sky for a minute or two. Then Anna said, "I saw something on the other side of the field."

"What did you see?" Tom asked.

"Lights. Like car lights that just turned off."

"You're sure?" Tom asked.

"That's what I saw," Anna said. "But I can't say for sure that it was a car."

Tom tapped Jamie on the shoulder. "Tell Chris not to land yet. Tell him to circle for five minutes, just to be sure."

Jamie turned on his wireless. "The favorite horse is scratched. The favorite horse is scratched. Bet on Number Five. Can you hear me, Chris? Bet on Number Five!"

"I hear you," the answer came back after a moment. "Number Five."

Tom tapped Claude's shoulder. "Turn your headlights on and off, but just once."

Out of the darkness, a car from across the field turned its headlights on and off, also just a single time.

"Probablement les adolescents faisant whoopee dans la voiture de papa," Claude whispered to Gilles.

"He was whispering. What did he just say?" Tom asked.

"Claude thinks it's some kids making whoopee in papa's car. He's probably right," Gilles whispered.

"I don't think so," Tom said.

After five minutes Jamie said, "The plane's coming in."

They all sat quietly and waited. When moonlight suddenly flashed across the wings of the Lysander just as it was about to touch down the ladies squeezed each others' hands. But before the plane came to a complete stop, the headlights from two cars across the field were turned on and machine-gun fire from both cars began firing at the plane.

"SHOOT THE LIGHTS OUT!" Tom shouted to Gilles and Claude. "GO FOR THE LIGHTS!" Gilles, Claude, and Jamie opened the car door and jumped out, moving away from the Mercedes as they began firing. They managed to knock out the headlights of both cars, but whoever was in them kept up a barrage on the plane.

"They haven't started firing on the Mercedes yet," Tom said to the women. "Lie down on the floor as low as you can. Hurry, please."

Chris, the pilot, was smart enough to move the plane forward and the enemy fire began to hit mostly air, but whoever was inside those cars started scattering their bullets left and right, trying to hit the men who were firing at them. Gilles got hit and swore in French. Tom jumped out of the Mercedes and dove onto the earth next to Gilles.

"I'm all right, Monsieur Tom," Gilles said. "They hit my left arm and leg, but I tell you I'm all right. I am not going to lose my wife and baby. Here, I loan you my machine gun if you promise to kill those bastards."

Tom grabbed it. On his belly he fired toward where the enemy fire was coming from. He heard one loud cry and a voice swearing in German, and then another shout from someone next to him. Claude and Jamie were now firing at the other car. Then the enemy gunfire stopped.

"Don't believe it, Monsieur," Gilles said. "They do this all the time. It's a trick. Get in your plane and get the hell out of here, please. Get in the plane. Vite! Vite!"

"You're bleeding," Tom said.

"So? You want a prize for knowing that? I'm all right, I tell you."

"I can't leave you like this," Tom said.

"And let everyone else die? What kind of the fucking jerk are you? Get out of here!" Gilles shouted.

Claude crawled up next to Gilles and said, "Mama will take care of her little boy. Please, Tom, do what Gilles say."

Tom ran to the Mercedes and rushed the women toward the plane. "Stay low, stay low," he kept shouting.

Jamie was there and helped Tom get the women inside the plane, then he got inside himself and held out his arm to help pull Tom up. "Go!" Tom yelled to the pilot. Just as it started to move, the Nazis opened fire again, trying to stop the plane from taking off. One bullet hit Tom in the chest and one hit his thigh. Jamie, with the help of Madame Lauro, pulled Tom in, but in the process Madame Lauro was hit in her shoulder several times. The pilot taxied to the end of the field, turned 180 degrees, and then drove full throttle down the length of the field. The Lysander lifted off and above the thickness of the forest.

THIRTY-ONE

Jamie had wired ahead to have separate ambulances for Madame Lauro and Tom. When the plane landed at RAF Wroughton airfield, which was fairly near the Queen Alexandra's Military Hospital in London, a car was also there to take the other women to accommodations that had been arranged for them. Anna insisted on going with Tom. She kissed Madame Lauro, who was being helped into her ambulance, gave a quick hug to the other ladies, and then climbed into Tom's ambulance. Two army doctors began working on Tom's wounds as soon as the ambulance left for the hospital.

Tom didn't try to talk while the doctors were working on him; he just squeezed Anna's hand. When the ambulance arrived at the hospital, a crew was waiting to lift him onto a gurney and take him to the operating room. Anna kept holding Tom's hand until she was told that she wasn't allowed to enter the operating room. She quickly took off her pink bow and placed it in Tom's hand. He waved good-bye with his other hand.

AN HOUR and twenty minutes later Tom was wheeled into the Intensive Care Unit, still half asleep from the anesthetic. Anna was told she could go in to see him, but only for a few minutes. The nurses had removed his clothes and covered him with a light-blue wrap before the doctors began working on him. When Anna went into the Intensive Care room, Tom's eyes were closed. She didn't want to disturb him, but he put out his hand for her.

"What's your name again?" he asked with a hoarse throat.

Anna was a little shocked by the question. "I'm Anna. Anna Rosenkilde. You remember me, don't you?"

"What color . . . is your hair?"

"Blonde," Anna said, realizing that Tom must almost be unconscious.

"Auburn," he said. "And you like to eat octopuses . . . and I have your heart," Tom said slowly as he opened his hand. It was still holding her pink bow. Anna leaned down and kissed him.

THIRTY-TWO

Col. William Hartley walked into Tom's hospital room in the afternoon two days later and saw Anna sitting near his bed. "Is he sleeping?" the colonel whispered.

"No, sir," Tom said as his eyes popped open. "Just give me a day or two, Colonel."

"He thinks he is all healed because they took out his catheter and allowed him to have scrambled eggs and tea for breakfast," Anna said. "When I got here I could see he was in pain, but he was so stubborn . . . he just wouldn't admit it. I told the nurse and she gave him some morphine and now he is all ready to jump out of an airplane again."

"Well, I've got some good news for you both and some bad news. Which do you want first, Lieutenant?"

"The bad news."

"The bad news is that a few people know more about

your physical condition than you do, so keep your mouth shut for awhile and listen to Anna. She's smarter than you are."

"I know that," Tom said.

"The good news is that Madame Lauro is going to be fine."

"Oh, thank goodness," Anna said.

"As for you, young man, the doctors told you that the bullet shot below your shoulder was this far away from your heart, but your leg is another story. Dr. Stein told me you're going to need some physical therapy for a few weeks and then your thigh'll be as strong as ever. Why aren't you smiling?"

"Do you know what happened to Gilles Piccard?"

"I'm terribly sorry, Tom. He died. But has it pierced your conscience yet that you saved four women from going to hell in a gas chamber?"

Anna held Tom's hand and said, "Tom, you told me in the plane that when you wanted to stay with Gilles he said, 'And let everyone else die?' Remember that, darling?"

"But it didn't have to happen. That's what's killing me."

"What the hell is that supposed to mean?" Colonel Hartley asked.

"How did the Nazis know that we were going to be in

111

that field and that a Lysander was going to pick us up at exactly ten p.m.?"

After a frustrated pause Colonel Hartley said, "I knew you were going to ask that. I just didn't think it would be this soon. I don't know the answer yet."

THIRTY-THREE

A week passed, during which time Tom grumbled to the nurses about being treated like an invalid, which he was, but after his last checkup Dr. Stein gave him permission to enter the real world again, provided he used a cane whenever he walked and that he also promised to continue his physical therapy classes. Tom agreed.

That night Tom and Anna finally had their long-awaited date at the Shepherdess Café. Alfred Hollingberry, their short and sweet waiter, was so touched to see them that he gave Tom a gentle hug and put his head against Tom's chest. "I would have done the same with you, Madam, if it weren't exactly impolite," Alfred said. "But may I shake your lovely hand?"

"Of course you may," Anna said.

"Now then, what shall we start with tonight, ladies and gents . . . some wonderful imitation Sancerre direct from Morocco?"

"Wonderful," Anna and Tom said together.

"Back in a jif," Alfred said as he hurried away.

Anna and Tom both reached out for the other's hands. When Anna's tears started dripping on Tom's hand, she quickly reached for her paper napkin. "Sorry," she said.

"Well, just like old times," Tom said. "You cry and I think about food."

"You said you wanted to marry me," Anna said with a little smile.

"I did. Good for you for remembering a little detail like that," Tom said.

"Why do you want to marry me?" Anna asked with her usual giggle.

"Uh-oh. Here comes one of the Danish games again. I want to marry you because I love you."

"Why?" she asked.

"Well . . . let me see . . . because you're very smart and you're extremely attractive, and you're compassionate . . . and you tell good jokes."

"Even better than your jokes?" she asked.

"No, not that good."

"Oh, you," Anna said and then gave him a little kiss.

"Anna, are you free tomorrow afternoon?"

"Yes, dear. Why? Have you got a special plan for us?"

"Not *that* plan, not yet anyway. I'll need another few days for that. Actually, I was very rude to the lady I met in Radar a few weeks ago. Her name is Sally Bedloe. She was very busy and I kept insisting that she tell me where you were, and she kept insisting that she didn't know who Anna Rosenkilde was. I didn't know then that you weren't allowed to tell me, or anyone else, where you worked. I want to apologize to that lady and show her that I've found you."

"Here's your Sancerre, folks. Nice and cold," Alfred said as he rushed in and poured the wine. Tom and Anna clicked glasses.

"To life," Anna said.

"To life," Tom said as he squeezed her hand.

TWENTY-FOUR

Tom walked into Radar headquarters holding Anna's hand. He had hoped it was lunch hour so he could see Sally Bedloe, and there she was, finishing a sandwich and a cup of tea.

"Miss Bedloe—I'm Lieutenant Cole. You met me once before, but I want to apologize for the way I spoke to you a few weeks ago when you insisted that you didn't know who or where Anna Rosenkilde was. Well, here she is!"

Sally got up with half a smile and walked over to shake hands with Anna. "I'm so happy to meet you, Miss Rosenkilde. Your young fellow can be a little rough at the edges, but I see that he's rather nice after all."

"It's a pleasure to meet you, Miss Bedloe," Anna said. "Please, eat your lunch. We didn't want to interrupt."

"You can call me Sally. Everyone else does. By the way, I heard about the death of your French friend and I want you to know how sorry I am, Lieutenant."

"That's very kind of you, Sally."

"Take care walking in this dark tunnel with a cane. It could be very dangerous," Sally said.

"Don't worry. I'll be fine in a few more days."

"Thank goodness. You'll watch out for him, won't you, dear?"

"I certainly will," Anna said.

THIRTY-FIVE

At 7:00 p.m. Sally Bedloe gathered up her few things, straightened her WAAF uniform, fluffed her hair a bit, and then said a quick good night to Delia Fine, her evening replacement.

"Good night, Sally," Delia said. "Going anywhere exciting tonight?"

"Oh, I'm much too tired, dear. I'll see you tomorrow," Sally said with a smile and walked out of Radar.

SALLY WALKED along Whitehall Road for a few minutes, then got on the bus that took her close to Trafalgar Square, which was only a mile away. After ten minutes she changed to another bus that took her near Carlos Place. When she got off the bus she walked along Mount Street for only a few yards and then into the tiny park that was home to the Church of the Immaculate Conception.

Sally walked into the church and sat down in the closest pew to the door. It was a small church, but its stained-glass windows were magnificent. It was truly a place of peace and beauty that allowed for quiet reflection, prayers, and tears. A giant stained-glass image of Jesus seemed to stare directly at Sally. Only two other people were in the church during her visit.

Twenty minutes later, after Sally had shed a few tears, she got up, left the beautiful church, and walked home.

THIRTY-SIX

April 1945

Tom sat with Col. William Hartley in his office.

"How are you feeling, Tom?"

"I'll race you on ice skates next week."

"If you were still in the hospital, maybe. But you'd probably still win. How's your girlfriend?"

"She's swell. Thank you for her leave of absence."

"My God, she deserved it," the colonel said.

"She's in a beauty parlor right now, sir, getting her hair dyed back to auburn."

"Good for her. What's up, Tom? Morris said it was urgent."

"Colonel, have you gotten any clues yet about how the Nazis knew we were going to be picked up on that soccer field?"

"So far, nothing. Why?"

"I have a small clue. It may be nothing, but it's about our friend Sally Bedloe from Radar."

"Tell me."

"I went to see her the other day, with Anna, to apologize for being so rude several weeks ago when she said Anna never worked with her. After my apology, she was very gracious, even complimented me for being rather nice after all, but then she said something that stuck in my brain all that night. She said, 'By the way, I heard about the death of your French friend and I want you to know how sorry I am.'"

"That's very strange," the colonel said.

"Could she have known about Gilles Piccard from anyone in SOE?"

"Absolutely not."

"How old is Sally?"

"Forty-five, forty-six. She's been with Radar close to ten years."

"Colonel, would you give me permission to go out at night without my military uniform?"

"I'm afraid you'd be arrested for indecency, Tom," Colonel Hartley said with a laugh.

"No, I mean—"

"I know what you mean. You want to wear your civilian clothes like any proper detective, and see where she goes at night."

"Yes, sir."

"She's very smart, you know, Tom. If she thinks you're following her she'd be on to something. For now, why don't you find someone else, someone she's never seen before? An ordinary-looking man or woman reading the paper or a magazine?"

"That's a good idea. Thank you, sir. Do you know where Sally lives?"

Colonel Hartley pressed the button on his intercom. "Morris, find out where Sally Bedloe lives, but say you're from the mail department, not SOE. I'll hold on . . . Go ahead, Morris, I'm listening . . . 117 Park Street. Thank you, Morris. Did you get that, Tom?"

"Yes, sir, 117 Park Street."

"And Tom, whoever you get to follow Sally home, tell him or her to look up at her roof and see if there's an aerial sticking out."

THIRTY-SEVEN

Tom waited at the Patisserie Tea Room on Shaftesbury Avenue, which was near Anna's beauty parlor. When Anna walked in with her brand-new auburn hair Tom's mouth dropped open. He got up quickly.

"I don't believe we've met. My name is Clark Gable and, forgive me for my audacity, but you are the most beautiful woman I've ever met."

"Thank you, Mr. Gable," Anna said.

"If I'm not being too bold, would you lie down with me . . . I mean, sit down with me and have a cup of tea?"

"I'd be happy to do either one."

"How gracious you are. By the way, is your auburn hair natural?"

"That's a woman's secret."

Tom helped her into her chair, kissed the back of her neck, and sat down next to her.

"You know, you're as beautiful as only one other person I know."

"Who is that, I wonder? And don't make me jealous."

"I met her in a café weeks ago but I don't remember her name. I think she's a Danish or Norwegian joke teller."

"Well, that's all right then. I love jokes, and brave men who save women's lives, and scones with hot tea."

Tom waved to the nearby waitress and ordered two cream teas.

"Now tell me how it went with Colonel Hartley," Anna said.

"He agreed to let me play detective, but I need your help."

"Tell me how."

"I need someone Sally doesn't know at all, to get on a bus with her and find out where she goes and what she does. If she changes buses, then change with her. If it's just to her house, I already know where she lives."

"I know the perfect person for you."

"Who?"

"Bertie Cresswell. She'd love to be useful and she'd be very good at it. She's also anxious to meet you because you telephoned her several times."

"Do you think she could come over here right now, so we can talk about some of the do's and don'ts, like what not to wear and how to stay inconspicuous?"

Anna got up and went to the phone. She talked for

almost two minutes and then rushed back. "Bertie's thrilled. She'll be here in fifteen minutes."

WHEN BERTIE walked into the Patisserie Tea Room, Anna stood up and waved. Tom got up a little slower because of his leg, but he was very happy about what he saw. Bertie was wearing exactly the kind of clothes he hoped she'd be wearing: a plain, woolen A-line skirt with a modest brown blouse. Though it was a sunny April day with some clouds that didn't seem threatening, she also had an umbrella wrapped around her arm just in case.

"Bertie," Anna said, "this is Tom, the handsome lieutenant with the beautiful reddish-blond hair you were talking to on the phone when I suddenly disappeared, and who came to get me and saved my life and who I love."

"Well, that's rather a long introduction, but I like it very much. May I give you a gentle hug, Lieutenant Tom?"

"I would be honored, Bertie." As they hugged each other Bertie whispered to Tom, "God bless you, young man."

"Sit down, Bertie," Anna said. "Would you like some tea?"

"Thank you, not right now. I want to hear my orders first."

"Well, they're not exactly orders," Tom said, "or else I'd have to put you on a salary."

Bertie laughed and said, "That's all right with me."

"I think what you chose to wear is perfect, Bertie, and all I want you to do is to get on a bus and behave normally, except that there is a woman—who we'll point out to you later—and we want you to get on the same bus that she does, and get off when she does. And if she takes another bus, then you get on that bus, too. Maybe it would be good if you read a magazine, just so long as you don't lose sight of her. Clear so far?"

"Certainly," Bertie answered.

"And when she gets off the bus and starts walking, walk behind her, not too close, but keep reading your magazine without losing sight of her, and tell me where she goes and if she does anything that seems unusual. And Bertie, if you follow her to her home, look up to see if there's an aerial on her roof that's sticking out. Is all this too complicated?"

"Not at all. Just as long as I don't have to shoot anybody."

THIRTY-EIGHT

At a few minutes past seven Sally came out of the tunnel and walked to the bus stop. She sat down on a bench, with Bertie, who was reading an *Express* magazine that had Lauren Bacall on the cover. No one else was waiting for the bus. Bertie looked up to see Tom across the street. He nodded a slow "yes." A man and woman came rushing up just as the fairly crowded bus arrived. Sally got on, then the man and woman, and then Bertie. And the bus took off.

Bertie was sitting a few rows behind Sally, and she casually glanced at her every few seconds, before going back to reading her magazine. When the bus reached Trafalgar Square several people got off, including Sally and Bertie. When the next bus came along it had MOUNT STREET printed in large letters above the driver's head. Sally got on with two young men and Bertie. When the bus reached Mount Street, Sally got off, followed by several well-dressed men who looked like bankers, and then by Bertie.

Bertie walked several yards behind Sally, stopping every now and then to look at a store window, the way she remembered Tyrone Power doing in the movies. Then Sally turned onto Mount Street's small but beautiful park with the Church of the Immaculate Conception.

Bertie had actually been here before, mostly to see the stained-glass windows in the church and the Garden of Remembrance outside, with the little cemetery near it. When she saw Sally go into the church, Bertie sat on a shadowed bench and waited for her to come out.

Fifteen minutes later, Sally came out wiping a few tears from her eyes, and began walking toward Hyde Park. Bertie didn't want to walk too closely behind her, but when they reached Park Street, Bertie put on her glasses and saw Sally enter a small town house. Bertie waited a few minutes, then walked past the townhouse, noted the number 117 over the door, and looked up at the roof. There was no aerial sticking out.

THIRTY-NINE

Colonel Hartley sat deep in thought as Tom waited in the chair opposite him. "It's a peculiar situation," the colonel finally said. "Strange if it should be Sally."

"If she hadn't told me how sorry she was about the death of my French friend I would never have suspected anything," Tom said.

"But we don't know if she's done anything but go to church and cry. I can't bring her in for that," the colonel said. "I'll tell you what—*you* follow her tonight, Tom. See for yourself where she goes and what she does. And if and when she goes home, keep looking for an aerial. She may have it in some cockamamy place. I'll be in my office. If she does start sending messages I'll have the RDF truck half a street away, waiting to intercept."

"Yes, sir."

"And if you want to be a detective, get some ordinary hat and keep it on your head. She'd know you by your hair even if you were sitting behind her."

FORTY

As Sally Bedloe came out of the tunnel that evening it began to drizzle. She took her bus to Trafalgar Square and another bus to Mount Street and then walked quickly to the Church of the Immaculate Conception. A man with a slight limp, who was carrying an umbrella and wearing a shabby, ordinary hat, walked into the church a minute after Sally did.

Sally sat down in the nearest pew. Tom sat two rows behind her and to one side, lowered his head in prayer, but kept looking up at her every few seconds.

Sally could have been praying, although Tom didn't see her lowering her head or moving her lips. She just kept staring at the large image of Jesus, as if she were hoping for an immaculate word or two. After a few minutes she turned to look at the three others in church, wiped the tears from her eyes, and walked slowly toward the door.

It was raining harder now. As she stepped outside,

Sally opened her umbrella and held it over her head. It not only kept her from getting soaked, but also prevented her from seeing very much around her as she walked home.

Tom, with an umbrella over his head and wearing his "ordinary," shabby hat, limped slowly behind Sally to 117 Park Street, hoping that *if* she started tapping messages once she was home, Colonel Hartley would have the RDF truck nearby, as he said he would, ready to intercept them. Tom looked up at Sally's roof from all different positions and angles, but he could see nothing that resembled an aerial.

Damp and hungry, Tom waited outside in the pouring rain for forty-five minutes. When the rain finally let up, he looked up at the roof one final time—and this time he saw what seemed like a small piece of aerial that was growing taller inch by inch. He finally realized that Sally must be jerry-rigging the aerial through an opening in her attic. He went to the nearest phone booth and called Colonel Hartley.

"Come to my office now," the colonel said. "You won't believe it. Well, yes you probably would. Come right away. You must be hungry. I hope you like tuna salad sandwiches and beer. Hurry up."

FORTY-ONE

At 9:00 p.m. Tom walked into the colonel's office, soaking wet, and was greeted warmly by the colonel.

"Sit down, take off those wet things, and help yourself to a sandwich. Do you like beer?"

"Yes, sir. I'd probably drink anything right now, hot or cold."

"Here," the colonel said as he handed Tom a large glass of Kingfisher beer from India. "Now listen to what your friend Sally wrote, translated from German into English. And don't choke."

> *130 Lancasters to Berlin,*
> *90 Halifaxes to Leipzig and Hamburg,*
> *79 Mosquitos to Wittstock Airfield*
> *8 Mosquitos to Schleswig Airfield*

All flights from the RAF will leave at nineteen hundred and thirty hours, tonight.

"How did you get this so fast?" Tom asked.

"Because she didn't use Enigma or any of the tricks we might have been looking for. She did what I told you she might try—just plain German. And it worked. I don't know for how long she would have continued if you hadn't caught her with that mistake about your French friend."

"She must be crazy."

"Or something else," the colonel said. "I've got another idea of why she did it, but I'll tell you later. Right now I think we've got to pull her in when she arrives for work tomorrow."

"Oh, she'll love that," Tom said.

"I used to be a lawyer in Missouri before this war, so my interrogation of Sally could be fairly easy or else she might be a real ballbuster, but I want you to be here when I question her."

FORTY-TWO

Sally came to work a minute or two before 10:00 a.m. as she always did. Two MPs were waiting nearby. When she opened the door, one of the MPs walked in.

"Miss Bedloe, you'll need to come with us to see Colonel Hartley," he said in a friendly way.

"Oh, I'm much to busy to see him now. Please tell the colonel that I'll drop by at lunchtime."

"I'm afraid that's impossible, ma'am," the MP said as the other MP stepped closer in case help was needed. "He wants to see you right now."

"Are you arresting me?"

"Please ask Colonel Hartley that, ma'am. Just come with us right now."

Sally's face turned a cold white, but she didn't argue anymore. She was ushered out of her office and along the tunnel to Colonel Hartley's office with an MP on either side of her. When they arrived, Sergeant Morris led them into the colonel's office. Tom was standing near the colonel. Sally stood still and stared at Colonel Hartley. The MPs were standing a few feet away from her.

"That's all right, fellas, you can wait in the outer office," the colonel said. The MPs saluted and left.

"Long time no see, Sally," Colonel Hartley said. "Won't you sit down?"

"I'd rather not," she said.

"I'd rather you did. Don't get tough with me, Sally, because I'll out-tough you. Now sit the *hell* down!"

Sally sat down.

"I believe you know Lieutenant Cole." Sally didn't answer or even look at Tom.

"Let's skip the usual shit, Sally, and tell me why you did it," the colonel said with a grim face. "No answer? All right, I'll tell you the consequences: twenty years in jail *if* you're incredibly lucky, but much more likely you'll be executed for betraying your country in time of war. I'll speak for you or against you depending on what you're willing to tell me today."

Sally stared at him, her face frozen.

"You may have cost the lives of thousands of men and women who were fighting this rotten war against Hitler."

"You don't understand Hitler or me."

"Well, I do understand why you cry in the Church of the Immaculate Conception," the colonel said.

Sally flushed red while her eyes looked to every corner

of the office. "How . . . how could you possibly know that?" she asked.

"Jesus told me."

"What are you talking about?" she said, almost screaming.

"Well he and I are both Jewish, you see, so he let me in on a few things. I can even tell that you're crying right now and he didn't say a word to me this time. He also told me that you were desperately in love with Sir Oswald Mosley. That man could sweep an audience off its feet, couldn't he? After his wife died he married his mistress in secret. In Joseph Goebbels's home. I believe Adolf Hitler was one of the guests. I admit that Mosley is a very handsome man, it's just that he is just another British asshole who loves Hitler. Then he left his wife and went to you, but dumped you after your three-year affair and went back to his wife. That must have broken your heart, not being able to make love with the man who fucked every other woman he met and wrote the book *Fascism*. I feel for you, Sally."

As her tears started to pour, she covered her face with her hands. "Do you have any idea why I cried in church?" she finally asked when she could speak clearly.

"Tell me," the colonel said.

"Because I knew that so many people might be killed . . . I knew that . . . but I thought I was doing something that would hasten peace."

"That's what Sir Oswald told you?"

"Yes. That's what he truly believed."

"Sally, I want you to talk to Lieutenant Cole now. He needs to know something that's extremely important. If you don't tell him the truth, I swear to God I won't be helping you when you stand in front of the judge who's going to decide if it's jail or execution for you."

Tom walked slowly up to Sally. Colonel Hartley sat down and listened.

"Sally, how did you know that my French friend had died?"

Sally looked away, then back, then away again. "I'm not going to ask you another time," Tom said.

"He didn't die," Sally said.

". . . What are you saying?"

"I was told to tell you that."

"Who told you?"

"Colonel Franz Stangl."

"Why?"

"He was afraid that if you knew your friend was still alive you'd try to contact him."

"Of course I would. Where is Gilles? *Look at me, Sally—* where is he?"

"He's in prison."

"Where?"

"In a village called Oberkirch, close to Alsace."

"Do you know if he's being tortured?"

"I don't think so. Colonel Stangl said they want your

friend to tell them more about other French Resistance fighters . . . how they communicate with each other, and how many there are in Alsace. They need him alive for now."

"Have they done anything to Gilles's family?"

"Colonel Stangl never mentioned them."

"Where do you send your messages, Sally?"

"To Freiburg, fifty miles from Alsace, because Freiburg can send them to other locations all over Germany."

Tom looked at Colonel Hartley, indicating that he was through with his questioning.

"All right, Sally, that's enough for today," Colonel Hartley said. "If what you've told us is true, I'll take it under consideration. I won't be the actual judge, you understand, but I might have some influence when the time comes. For now, I want you to ask for the things you need from your home. One of our WAAFs will take your key, and you just tell her where your things are and what you want. You'll be in a special location. Not luxurious, but not so bad as a prison. It's a small house and has a decent bed and bathroom."

Colonel Hartley pressed the intercom.

"Morris, ask the MPs to escort Miss Bedloe to the Internment House and please ask someone from WAAF headquarters to meet her there."

"Yes, sir," Morris answered.

"And ask Captain Pryce to come in here right now."

"Yes, sir." Morris answered.

Colonel Hartley turned off the intercom and looked at Tom. "I know what the hell you're thinking, so don't look at me with that sour puss. That's why I asked for Captain Pryce."

"What in the world are you talking about, Colonel?"

"I'm talking about getting your friend out of that prison."

FORTY-THREE

Captain Pryce and Tom sat with Colonel Hartley around the little table where the colonel always served tea or coffee.

"It's called Death Camp Oberkirch," Captain Pryce said. "It's located near a railroad and it's surrounded by thick trees. It's run by SS Obersturmführer Franz Stangl, a veteran of the Nazi euthanasia program. In Gilles Piccard's case I'm sure Miss Bedloe was right—Stangl will want to keep him alive, at least for a while, in order to get more names of French Resistance fighters."

"Do we still have agent Brian Lewis in the Alsace neighborhood?" Tom asked.

"Yes, we do," Captain Pryce said.

"And are you still in touch with Claude Breton?" Tom asked.

"We can be," Captain Pryce said.

"I have an idea, Colonel, if you'll let me go there," Tom said.

"Go where?"

"To Camp Oberkirch."

"Stop it now!" the colonel said. "You're not going any-where. You're just here to help us figure out this thing. You're a cripple, for Christ's sake!"

Tom suddenly got up and did a little two-step, soft-shoe dance.

"All right, all right—excuse me, Mr. Astaire. What brilliant idea have you come up with this time?"

"Does Brian Lewis speak German?"

"He was born in Alsace," Pryce said.

"If Brian and Claude dressed as Nazi soldiers, and if they brought me into Camp Oberkirch dressed as a Frenchman and then told whoever was in charge at the entrance that they found this French Resistance fighter who was about to blow up something or other . . . I think I'd get in."

"That probably could work," Captain Pryce said, look-ing at the colonel to guage his approval.

Colonel Hartley stared at Tom. "You want to try your hardest to get into a death camp . . . while everyone else in the death camp wants to get out. Damn good idea! But tell me, how do you plan on getting you and your friend out of there? What happens if, by some little piece of bad luck, neither one of you *ever* gets out?"

"I can't tell you exactly how, sir, but I think there must be a lot of French Resistance fighters imprisoned in

Oberkirch. With ten or eleven men who are still strong enough, maybe we could start another French Revolution. All the other prisoners would then hopefully join us in our fight to get out."

Colonel Hartley put his hand over his mouth until his heart slowed down. "Either this man is dead or my watch has stopped."

"What does that mean?" Tom asked.

"It means you should have been in the movie *Monkey Business* with the Marx Brothers. You're brave and you're smart, and you're a damned good officer, and I don't want to send you off to your death, do you understand that?"

FORTY-FOUR

Anna's tears were dripping into her glass of wine in the Shepherdess Café.

"You can't, you can't. Please darling, don't go there, unless you take me with you.... You know how tough I was in Denmark and how good I was in Alsace. I can help you, and I don't know what I'd do if you were there and I was in London waiting for you to come back to me."

"I would take you with me, darling, if they let women into Oberkirch. But it's one of those stuffy, exclusive kind of men-only places. And all the men would be flirting with you every single day, and I'd be so jealous I'd start to cry and I'd probably write my mother that I wanted to come home."

Anna started to giggle while she cried. "That's not funny," she said. "And I tell better jokes than you."

"Well, let's hear a few. I could use a good laugh right now."

"I don't feel like telling jokes. You don't love me anymore."

Tom pulled his chair next to hers, put his arm around her shoulders, and kissed her for such a long time that a crowd started to assemble around them. When Tom and Anna looked up, the crowd yelled, "Well done!"

"I'm so embarrassed," Anna said.

"Thank you ladies and gents," Tom said to the crowd. "Very kind of you. Our next performance will be in approximately ten minutes." The audience applauded. Some were holding hands as they went back to their seats.

Tom held Anna's hand and looked into her beautiful blue-green eyes. "After what he's gone through for me, I just want to get Gilles out, Anna. I think the war is coming to an end soon and chances might be better now than they would have been a few months ago. Please trust me, dear. I will come back. If I didn't it would ruin our marriage. So show me how tough you can be by staying here and waiting for me."

Anna put her head on his chest and said in Danish, *"Okay, min kaereste mand."* (Okay, my dearest husband.)

FORTY-FIVE

Brian Lewis held one of Tom's arms and Claude Breton held the other as they approached the main gate to Camp Oberkirch. Brian and Claude were wearing dusty German uniforms. Tom was wearing typical French working clothes, with patches sewn over a few holes in his pants. He struggled and yelled at his "German captors" as he tried to get away.

"Laissez-moi aller vous connards muet. Je n'etais pas exploser quoi que ce soit!" (Let me go, you dumb assholes. I wasn't trying to blow up anything!)

A guard came up to them. "What have you got here?" he said in German.

"A piece of junk. We caught him trying to blow up the railroad tracks nearby," Brian answered in German.

"Give him to me. I know how to handle his kind," the guard said. He slapped Tom three times across his face and kicked him in the balls. Tom slumped over.

"You both did good," the guard said. Brian and Claude watched as the guard grabbed Tom's arm and pulled him through the gate and into the death camp.

Tom, still in terrible pain, was pulled past the factory where POWs were working. He also saw that Oberkirch was a much larger camp than he had imagined.

"You'll soon be in the factory with the other shits, and you'd better not try to work slow or I promise you will regret the punishment," the guard said in German.

They arrived at several rows of POW barracks. Tom was pushed into the first one, which turned out to have hot and cold running water. He was sure that the beds were just old army beds that had begun to fall apart.

As the guard was leaving he said, "Obersturmführer Franz Stangl will see you shortly and you had better behave with him," he said in German.

"Merci bien," Tom muttered.

Twenty minutes later, after Tom washed his face and mouth with cold water and sat on his lumpy bed, Franz Stangl walked in. Tom stood up.

"What is your name?" Stangl asked in English.

"Mon nom est Charles Aznavour."

"Oui? Monsieur Charles Aznavour? Voulez-vous chantez 'La Mer' pour moi, s'il vous plaît," Stangl said in perfect French.

Shocked that Stangl could not only speak perfect French

but also knew of Aznavour, Tom wasn't sure what to do. So he began to sing: *"La mer, qu'on voit danser le long des golfes clairs—"*

"That's enough. So you speak French, a little German, and . . . some English perhaps?"

"Yes, sir, because I live in Alsace," Tom said.

"I see," Stangl said. "Do you have many other Resistance friends from Alsace?"

"I teach music, sir. I'm not a fighter, I play the cello," Tom said.

"I see. Come with me, Monsieur Charles Aznavour," Stangl said as he walked out of the barracks.

Two guards were waiting outside to assist Stangl in case of trouble. With great difficulty, Tom tried to walk standing straight up as he followed him to the large factory that he had passed on the way to the barracks. Once inside the factory, Tom saw that hundreds of POWs were making long pipes on metal tables.

"Over here!" Stangl shouted.

As Tom approached Stangl, he saw Gilles Piccard facing him. Gilles's body and face were so thin and his eyes looked as if they, too, were standing at attention, until he saw Tom. But Gilles didn't make a sound.

"Do you know this man?" Stangl asked Tom.

"I don't know him, sir . . . I think I met him once or twice," Tom answered.

"Where?"

"In Alsace, sir. Waiting in line at the butcher shop, probably."

"Do you know his name?"

"I only met him once, maybe twice. We didn't exchange names."

"And what is your real name, Monsieur Aznavour?" Stangl asked with the hint of a smile. "I'll give you one minute to remember it."

"Edmond Rochefort," Tom answered.

"Good," Stangl answered. "Now, I'll ask you again. . . . Do you know this man?"

"I don't know him, sir. I met him, I think in a butcher shop or in a line someplace, at the cinema maybe. I don't honestly remember."

"Gilles Piccard, do you know this man?"

"As he says, sir, I think we did meet someplace, but I don't know where it was. He is certainly not a friend of mine, if that's what you mean."

"No, what I mean is, do you kill German soldiers together or blow up railroad tracks together. Things like that?"

"If I knew him, I would say so right now, so I could avoid any more beatings," Gilles said, looking Tom in the eye.

Stangl looked at them both as if he were deciding. "All right Piccard, go back to work. Rochefort, go with those two guards and get your prison clothes. I wouldn't want you to ruin your beautiful pants."

WHEN TOM came back to his barracks that night, after eating something called dinner, he found a cello resting near his bed. A few minutes later Commandant Stangl walked in carrying a bow.

"The idiots brought you the cello I had in my office, but they forgot the bow. The cello was from one of the prisoners we had who died a few weeks ago. Maisky was a good musician. Would you please play something for me . . . Bach, if you are acquainted with his work?"

Tom took the bow from Stangl, sat on the edge of his lumpy bed, and placed the cello between his legs. He felt the strings several times, looked up at Stangl, and then played the Prelude from Bach's "Cello Suite No.1."

Stangl didn't smile and didn't look at Tom as he played. He just turned his head to one side as he listened. When Tom finished, Stangl got up, nodded his head up and down a few times and said, "Thank you. I'll have my officers pick up the cello and bow. *Auf Wiedersehen.*"

FORTY-SIX

During his second day of working in the factory, Tom met nine friends of Gilles Piccard. Each one passed by slowly and said, *"Bonjour La Mer."* Tom smiled and realized that the nine men who greeted him must have been Gilles's French Resistance friends.

While Tom was working, if it was clear that no one was near enough to hear him, Tom spoke softly to one of the friends. "Why in the world are we installing pipes onto the ceiling and through a wall?"

"In order to kill people in the gas chamber they've built next door," the friend answered. "The gas is supposed to go through these fucking pipes and through the wall, but I don't think it will go through because we've been loading stones into the pipes to block the gas. If you want to help us, then make sure the bastards don't see you putting stones in the pipes."

A guard came by and said, "If you talk to each

other again instead of working, you won't get food tonight."

"That would be a pleasure," Tom said to himself.

WHEN SIX hundred male prisoners sat down to eat dinner in the commissary that night, Tom decided it was safe enough to sit near Gilles.

"One of your friends told me about filling the pipes to block the gas," Tom said softly while he ate his small share of stale bread with a thin and grainy sour soup. "It sounds like a good idea but where do we get the stones?"

"On the ground all over the camp," Gilles said. "Put the bigger ones in your pants and the smaller ones in your shoes."

OVER THE next few days, Tom's body got weaker. He thought he would become stronger from all the pipe lifting, but maybe building muscle takes more time. Instead of sleeping better, each night he was sleeping less—partly from exhaustion and partly from dreams of Anna, looking so beautiful, and then being whipped and raped by Nazis, which would cause him to wake up immediately. Then he would lie in his rotten bed wondering if he would ever see her again.

On the day of the big gas chamber test, all the prisoners were given a short break and allowed a cup of water while Stangl's next-in-command, Kurt Hubert Franz, took joy in explaining to the prisoners what was going to happen.

"Thirty Jewesses have undressed in a clearing in the woods, which has been roofed over," Franz said with a smirk. "Right now they are being herded by the SS into our new gas chamber. When the doors have been closed, we shall see if all of our hard work will be successful. Come outside," he announced.

The prisoners were guided out of the factory by the guards and placed in front of the gas chamber doors, which had been closed. After fifteen minutes the doors were opened and the women's corpses were removed by a group of Jewish workers. Eighteen-year-old Katrina Deen was the youngest victim. Some of the prisoners threw up. As Tom watched the women's bodies being carried past him, he felt so humiliated that he couldn't move his feet, until a guard finally shoved him into motion with the butt of his rifle.

TOM LOADED more and more stones into the pipes. Whenever mealtime came, Tom felt that the food was almost not worth eating. Some of the prisoners went outside and ate the grass. After two weeks Tom began eating grass regularly. Soap, toothpaste, and toothbrushes were unheard of.

Tom came into contact with what he called a few of

the Jewish Lads, who were treated brutally by the officers. Tom, with Gilles's nine friends, would steal any food they could and leave it hidden where it could be seen by the Jewish workers in the factory. If Tom and his friends were caught stealing, they knew that the punishment would be severe.

One afternoon, while Tom, Gilles, and the nine Resistance friends were working in the technical camp along with some other prisoners, an SS officer started beating a particularly frail Jew, who was maybe sixty years old. Then he was pushed into one of the other prisoners. The Jew was so outraged that he walked up to the SS officer, insulted him, and then spat in his face. The officer was so outraged that he quickly pulled out his gun, but when he saw that the other prisoners surrounded the Jew and wouldn't move without a fight, he returned his gun to its holster.

Tom became aware of partisans from the local town who were willing to accept a small amount of money to work each day in the camp. They were also willing to sabotage the Nazi efforts. One of the partisans offered to smuggle in some radio parts—which Tom was desperate to get—in return for chocolate and cigarettes, which the partisan craved and which a few prisoners—who were not French or Jewish—received from their families.

After a few days, Tom believed he had enough radio parts to send messages. But on his way back to bed Tom saw that all of the prisoners in the area were being searched. He couldn't just drop the radio parts that the partisan gave him because it would certainly be seen, and he couldn't run because he was being watched by an SS officer, the same officer who Tom had seen beating up the frail Jewish man.

The radio parts were discovered and Tom was grabbed by a guard and taken before a senior officer who was sitting behind a large desk. When he refused to give away the partisan's name, Tom was beaten and thrown into a cell, where his hands were tied together behind his back and then suspended from the ceiling for thirty minutes. He was certain he was going to die. But despite having several fractured ribs, plus hands and arms so injured that he was afraid it was the end of cello playing forever, he was taken back to his barracks and allowed to live.

Why? Tom couldn't understand it. There was no reason. When he lay down on his bed, the only image that came into his mind was Anna's pink bow.

FORTY-SEVEN

Given one day to rest, Tom was ordered back into the factory. Franz Stangl greeted him that night, just after Tom came back to his bed to lay down.

"I heard that you were disturbed by the killing of those thirty Jewesses. Is that right?"

"Yes," Tom said without fear.

"Here is a lesson for you to learn. Poles, Gypsies, Dutch, French, and Russians were not killed. But Jewish Poles, Jewish Gypsies, Jewish Dutch, Jewish French, and Jewish Russians will be eliminated. You can tell that to your friends."

"I will. I promise you that," Tom said.

"Good," Stangl said. "And would you like to know why you're still alive?"

Tom sat up. "Yes, I would like to know why."

"First of all, on the day we met you told me that your name was Charles Aznavour, whose music I am very familiar with. He is also Jewish. I'm sure you knew that, but your arrogance probably assured you that I wouldn't. Second, the guards told me that you are circumcised, so I knew for sure that you were Jewish. Third, because you helped feed the Jewish workers. And fourth because you got the radio parts from a partisan whose name you were brave enough not to reveal."

Tom was astonished by what he was hearing, but even more baffled by why he was still alive.

"So—" Franz Stangl said like an egotistical history professor, "why are you here? Why am I even talking to you? The simplest reason is because I admire you for your courage, even though I'm sure you hate me. But the true reason . . . is that, like a good German, I love music. When you played Bach for me I realized that you were quite a good cellist. And when I found out that my next in command had you suspended with your hands tied behind your back, I ordered him to have the rope cut down immediately. So you don't have to thank me for being alive. . . . You must thank Schumann, Beethoven, Wagner, Mendelssohn, Bach, Mozart, and Richard Strauss. They were also good Germans, and they are the reason why you are a living Jew in a German concentration camp. *Auf Wiedersehen.*"

FORTY-EIGHT

The next day, a German engineer declared that they were going to carry out a pressure test on the pipes that would carry the gas to the gas chamber. The prisoners stood frozen. "*Oh, merde!*" Gilles said. "No chance these pipes are going to pass the test. Not now with all those stones we've stuffed in there." All the prisoners looked at the smiling faces of the officers. "Those bastards know what we've done," Gilles said.

The officers started lining up all of the prisoners against a wall, ready to shoot them when the test failed. Some of the prisoners started to pray, some hugged each other. Then the sound of the air raid siren suddenly blasted throughout the factory. All of the officers and guards, and then the prisoners, ran out of the factory and into the air raid shelter outside. When they heard the bombs starting to fall, Tom, Gilles, and their French Resistance friends sat together in the shelter, holding hands.

After twenty-five minutes, the attack was over. Every-one went outside and the prisoners saw that the bombs that hit the factory had also blown up the gas chamber. Amid the quiet, *"Bravos"* and *"Fantastiques"* whispered by his friends, the only words that went through Tom's head were: *Colonel Hartley.*

The camp was being bombed regularly now, day after day. Tom and Gilles and their friends stole pistols and ammunition from the dead and dying officers and guards. They shot the ones near them who were still alive. Their strategy was to kill as many of the SS as they could and then walk out of the main gate, except Gilles was discov-ered missing. Tom feared for the worst until Gilles re-turned looking frustrated.

"Where the hell have you been?" Tom asked. "I was afraid you were killed or captured."

"I went to Commandant Stangl's office to shoot him, but he wasn't there. Let's get out of here."

When they walked out of the prison and into the open camp, there were more SS officers and guards waiting to fire at all the prisoners on sight. With Gilles's help, Tom ran toward the woods as fast as he was able to, but he kept falling.

Brian and Claude shouted to them from the woods: "Here! Over here! . . . To your right! DON'T STAND UP—THEY CAN SEE YOU IF YOU STAND— CRAWL!"

Brian continued screaming while he and Claude fired their submachine guns at every SS officer and Nazi guard in sight.

Tom and Gilles tried to crawl on their knees, but the bullets were coming too close to their bodies. "LOWER!—CRAWL ON YOUR BELLIES!" Brian shouted.

"Sur le ventre!" Claude yelled in French.

Tom and Gilles began to crawl on their bellies as fast as they could, pulling their bodies forward with their hands and pushing with their feet without raising their bodies. They inched their way until they finally reached the beginning of the woods, but they kept crawling until they heard Claude yell, "Bravo!" When they were in far enough, they both stood up and hugged each other. Then the four men made their way deeper into the woods.

Three hundred of the six hundred prisoners who tried to escape made it out of the camp that day and into safety.

FORTY-NINE

Tom was sitting on a table in the doctor's office a week later, wearing only his underwear, when Colonel Hartley walked in.

"You look a wreck," the colonel said.

"Thank you, sir. And thank you for sending the RAF to bring us home."

"You're very welcome," Colonel Hartley said. "You're a lucky son of a gun. Doc says your ribs are fractured, not broken."

"I knew that, Colonel. I was a medic, remember? What about my hands?"

"He said that if you take it easy for a while and start eating again you'll be as fit as a fiddle. Maybe even a cello."

"Colonel . . . how did you know where and when to bomb?"

"Well . . . partly because I'm smart, partly because I'm lucky, and mostly because I was in touch with Brian Lewis every day, and he told me where he *thought* the gas chamber was. You and I were both lucky that he was right and that the pilot didn't miss the target. The other places we bombed were technical buildings, nothing near where they kept the prisoners. Oh, and Brian told me to tell you that while Gilles was in prison his family was never touched, so you can relax about that."

"I'm terribly grateful to you, Colonel."

"You're more than welcome, son. So what are your plans?"

"To be with the woman I love."

"Not a bad plan. By the way, if you should ever get tired of being happy you can always work with me in my office. I could use a fellow like you, with ideas that could never work."

"Thanks for the compliment."

"Perhaps you'd like to be a captain now. It must be pretty boring just being a lieutenant for over five months?"

"Thank you, but no, sir. Just being a lieutenant is fine with me until the war is over."

"It's going to be over sooner than you think, Tom."

FIFTY

The Shepherdess Café—May 25th, 1945

"You look so much better, darling. The bruise over your eyebrow looks almost gone, and a little color is coming back to your cheeks."

"As long as I don't frighten you again."

"You didn't frighten me. Not at all. It's just—when I first saw you get off that plane, I was—"

"A little frightened?"

"Yes, I was a little . . . Oh, now you make jokes again. I'm the joke teller."

"Don't cry, Anna. Everything's fine, as long as you still love me, even if I'm not very pretty."

"But you are very pretty."

"No, I mean—even when I'm not very good-looking."

"You are very good-looking, *min elskede . . . min lille kaereste.*"

"Uh-oh. Now you're talking Danish again and I don't know what you said."

"Nothing of importance. I was just thinking that Alfred should be here with our food any minute now and you must be very hungry."

"You little liar. You couldn't have said all that with four Danish words."

"Well, I just added added a few more words and now look—here he is."

Alfred Hollingberry came bouncing up to them, holding a platter with fish and vienna steak and potatoes and salad. He also had another bottle of the Moroccan imitation Sancerre under his arm. As he approached he started singing as he dished out their food:

As I stroll down Pic Piccadilly in the bright morning air,
All the girls will declare, he must be a millionaire.

"And how how are we doin' folks? A little hungry I hope."

"Oh, yes," Anna said.

"Very good salmon tonight, and fairly good 'sort of steak.' Shall I pour your fake Sancerre now?"

"Yes, please," Tom said.

"We missed the both of you so much. It's grand ta see you back, sir."

"Thanks, Alfred."

"Now, I'll leave you alone so you can enjoy yourselves," Alfred said and bounced away.

"Tom, you're crying. What's wrong, dear?"

"Nothing . . . Nothing's wrong, darling. I haven't had a breakdown. It's just that . . . I didn't think I'd ever see you again. And here you are with Alfred and a fake steak again. Isn't it wonderful?" Tom said as he took a hanky out of his pocket and wiped his eyes.

Anna came over and sat on Tom's lap. "It is wonderful," she said and kissed him nine or ten times. He held the pink bow in her hair as he tried to return her kisses.